HOOD SUPREME 4

MZ. LADY P

MZ. LADY P PRESENTS, LLC

Hood Supreme 4

After a long day of getting the girls ready for their next recital, I was beat. All I wanted to do was get home so I could take a nice hot bath, plus I missed my son. I had been away from G-Baby all day long. All he does is cry, but I love being with my crybaby. I never knew I could love someone as much as I do my son. Givenchy says I'm going to make him soft. I don't care. I just want to give him all the love I have to give. That love from a parent is everything. I know how it feels to be neglected by a parent. As long as I have blood flowing through my veins, I'm going to make sure my children feel loved. Being a mom to him and Gianna completes me. I never thought I would see the day where I would race home to my family.

Hearing the siren and seeing the flashing lights made me quickly pull to the side of the road. I immediately reached for my license and registration. I really didn't understand why I was being pulled over in the first place. I hadn't run any signs or lights, and I had my proper signals on as well as my seatbelt. This officer had no reason to stop me. I damn near jumped out of my skin the way he banged on my window.

"License and registration, please!"

"Why am I being pulled over? I didn't do anything, officer."

I quickly handed my documents to him. He quickly walked off, and I observed him getting back inside of his patrol car. I bit down on my bottom lip nervously because it started to take too long.

After about ten minutes of waiting, I observed another patrol car pull up. At that time, an officer and a K-9 dog started walking toward my car. I noticed the officer who had pulled me over started walking with them. My heart felt like it was about to jump out of my chest. I didn't understand why they needed a dog. Something was off with this traffic stop. I regretted not calling Givenchy when the officer first pulled me over. Now it was too late because they had come back to the car.

"Step out of the car, ma'am!"

"For what?"

"Please don't resist! Step out of the car, ma'am!" This time he spoke with anger in his voice.

I quickly got out of the car and walked me off to the side, afraid he might shoot me. The dog immediately started to go crazy sniffing by the trunk. I knew that dog had to be fucked up or something. There were no drugs of any kind in my car.

"Jackpot! It's must be over twenty keys in here."

"What? No! No! Somebody put that shit in there. Please let me call my fiancé!" I was crying, begging and pleading, but he forcibly put me in cuffs. He was reading me my rights, but it's as if my whole body was numb. Somebody had planted that shit inside of my trunk. Who in the fuck would do some shit like that to me? On the ride to the jail, all I could do is think about Givenchy and the kids. What would *they do with me being locked up? This shit was so fucked up. Why does bad shit keep happening?*

One Week Later

I was about to lose my fucking mind sitting in the jail cell. Shit was all bad. The judge held me without bail. There was no telling how long I was about to be here. The whole family had been trying to keep me calm each time I called. All I want to do is go home to G and the kids. I'm not supposed to be locked up. Givenchy needed to handle this shit so that I could get the fuck outta here. To make matters worse, my ass is knocked up again. I found out when I came through intake. There was no way I could have a baby behind bars.

"Let's go, Mills. You have a special visit!" *I hurried up and got up from my bunk. Givenchy told me he was going to get us a visit. All I need to do is see him and touch him. It will make me feel so better about the situation.*

"Do you know if it's my fiancé?"

"Sorry. I don't know who it is."

We continued to walk down a long corridor until we came to a small door. He removed the cuffs and basically pushed me inside. The moment I locked eyes with Melissa in the same orange jumpsuit as mine, I knew this was about to be some bullshit.

"My have the mighty fallen. Look at you, daughter, you're a reflection of your mother." *She laughed as she flamed up a Newport.*

"I'm nothing like you."

"Yes, you are. That's the problem. You're walking around thinking you're better than me when you're really just like me. I mean, look, we're dressed just alike."

"Orange fits you just well. Let me out of here!" *I started* banging on the door, but it never opened. Melissa got up from where she was sitting and got so far in my face our noses were damn near touching.

"Do you think I built my life just so that you could make it crumble? From the moment I birthed your ass, I knew you would fuck my life up. Now look at you. Talk that big shit now about what your man can do! Newsflash, that nigga don't run shit in here. As a matter of fact, I run this whole tier, and you will fall in line like the rest of the bitches. You want to go against me for Team Supreme! Game on, daughter! Always remember, I brought you in this world, and I have the power to take you out!"

Before I could say anything, the door opened, and in walked about four female inmates. I didn't really have a chance to scream or do anything. They all just started beating the fuck out of me. I tried my best to fight back, but I was outnumbered. It seemed like the punches and kicks would not stop coming. I could feel blood dripping into my eyes, so everything was blurry. I felt myself giving up and just falling to the floor. I could hear G in my head, repeating his motto.

Chin up and chest the fuck out!

It gave me the strength to stay standing for a little while longer. I fought like hell, trying not to let them get me down. All the fight I had in me was gone when one of them pulled out a blade and sliced my face. I hit the floor like a ton of bricks, and the beating stopped. As I stared into Melissa's dark eyes, I vowed to survive and make her pay for everything she's done to me. This Hood Supreme shit was about to get real fucking heavy around this motherfucker!!!!

ONE

MIYANI

SIX MONTHS LATER

I grimaced as I stared in the mirror at the scar going down the right side of my face. My appointment for plastic surgery was coming soon, and I couldn't wait. I was happy Givenchy had got me one of the best surgeons to fix the shit. When I was laid up in the hospital, I cried every day. Nobody would let me see my face, and that shit was scary. Just thinking about how them bitches jumped me hurts like hell. I've never been jumped on or beat on like that. Melissa was trying to prove a point, and sadly she got her point across. That shit broke my spirit and my heart. I'm not surprised that she had that done to me. It's more so the way she looked on as they did the shit. There I was back to asking why she's doing this to me. To this day, I still don't understand.

It's been six months since that shit happened and it feels like it happened yesterday. The best part about all of this is that I'm free and home with my family. All the charges were dropped against me after a month of being in jail. I've never asked why or how. I already know Givenchy handled that shit. He doesn't talk about it, but I know he's on the hunt for Melissa. I am as well. He just doesn't know that. I'm happy he wants to fight all my battles for me. At the same time, he must allow me to fight my battles. He's been treating me like a weak ass bitch, and I don't like it.

With so much going on, I've been in a really bad head-space. I haven't really been working on any of the projects the family has going on. I've hired a manager full time to run my dance studio. I've lost my passion for everything, and it sucks. The hardest part about being depressed is smiling for the world while you're crying on the inside. I don't want to sound selfish or like an ungrateful bitch. However, I miss the normal life that I had. Things were so simple before I fell in love with Givenchy. Loving and choosing him has cost me my sanity. Nothing is normal about this life. He provides and loves me like no other. At the same time, I'm not the Miyani I fell in love with. Honestly, I don't think I'm the Miyani G fell in love with. Things are different between us. I don't know what it is, but we are definitely not the same people that fell in love at first sight.

Regardless of the sudden disconnect, I know he loves me and feels terrible about everything that has happened. The only thing I can do is keep the faith and believe that this, too, shall pass.

"WHERE ARE YOU GOING?" Givenchy asked as he walked inside of our bedroom.

"Furniture shopping with my sister and Dream." I slipped on my heeled boot and started placing on my jewelry.

"Nah! You can furniture shop online. I don't want you out of the house."

"Gunna or Butta can escort me."

"Gunna and Butta had to make a run to Dallas this morning."

"I'll be safe," I lowkey said with an attitude.

This man had been keeping me in the house. At first, I was cool with that, but now I want some air. My hair was hiding my scar, so I was comfortable going out in public.

"I said, NO!" This nigga had yelled at my ass like he was crazy. My head spun around so quick.

"I am not your child. Don't yell at me, Givenchy! I said, I'll be safe. I'm going furniture shopping."

He pinched the bridge of his nose like he was trying to calm down, which was a good thing because he needed to not say the wrong fucking thing to me.

"No! You're not my child. My kids listen to me. Your ass is trying the fuck out of me right now! This is why your ass got pulled over in the first place! I distinctly told your ass not to go anywhere without telling me. You knew not to make a move without an escort. That shit would never have happened to you in jail had your hard-headed ass listened!" he yelled at me so hard that I damn near jumped out of my skin. The veins in his neck were protruding, and his fist was balled up.

"Nah! That shit wouldn't have happened if I would never have got with your ass. Life was simple when all I did was dance. Since the day I become a part of this shit show called Team Supreme, shit has been fucked up."

I wasn't trying to hurt him, but the look in his eyes said I did. Maybe I went too far with that last comment. By the same token, I'm tired of all these fucking rules and demands. I waited for him to say something, but he didn't.

Instead, with brutal force, G snatched my Team Supreme chain from my neck. I felt it dig in my neck as it ripped. Tears welled up in my eyes, but I didn't allow them to fall.

"Why would you do that?" I asked somberly. Before I knew it, he was grabbing my hand and forcefully removing my engagement ring.

"You don't need to be affiliated with anything that fucks up your life. Since life with me has been so fucked up, we can end this shit now. The wedding is off. Give me my fucking ring back! I'm walking around this motherfucker being a good nigga to your ungrateful ass. All I've ever wanted to do was give you a good life. Obviously, I haven't been doing a good job. From this point forward, I don't give a fuck what you do, but nothing will happen to my son or daughter. You can leave this house or stay. I don't give a fuck. Just make sure you don't say shit to me and stay the fuck out of my way. I'm walking around this bitch, killing everything moving for your ass, and this the thanks I get."

"Givenchy, please!"

"Didn't I say don't say shit to me!" G gritted and stared me down like an animal, and I was his prey. All I could do was cower under him.

As he headed out of the room, he punched the wall. I quickly slammed the damn door and locked it. The tears flowed down my face like a raging river. Things were not supposed to be this way between us. My heart ached as I stared at my now bare ring finger. I felt like my death was imminent behind not marrying Givenchy. My phone rang repeatedly, but I couldn't pull myself together to answer. Instead, I undressed and crawled back into my bed. If I wasn't depressed before, I was definitely depressed now.

IT HAD BEEN two weeks since Givenchy and I fell out. What I thought was something that we could fix quickly, turned out to be something far bigger. I really thought that he was just upset for the moment and would come back to apologize. My dumb ass is still waiting for that apology. This nigga seriously broke up with me. The fact that we haven't spoken a word to one another in two weeks has me fucked up in the head.

It's been a couple of times I wanted to apologize, but he would just ice grill me. The look of disgust upon his face makes me feel low. Givenchy's punishing me, and the shit hurts like hell. I just have to let this shit pass and try to live my life. The shit is hard trying to do when Givenchy is my life.

In my absence, a lot of paperwork had piled up, and bills needed to be handled on the property. It was as if Givenchy said fuck everything.

My phone was going off crazy with notifications. I knew they were from the family. I had been dreading sending out texts that our wedding was off, but I had no choice but to. The day had arrived for everyone to get fitted for their dresses and tuxes. I had booked us a private fitting at the boutique for it. It wouldn't be fair for me to allow them to think the wedding was still on. Givenchy is extremely private, so I know he hasn't said a word.

"What the fuck is wrong with you? Why are you calling off the wedding?"

"Hello to you too, Dream." I looked up from the paperwork that I was working on.

She had bussed in my office at Supreme Suites like a madwoman. I wouldn't be surprised if Lexx and Gavin aren't too far behind her.

"Don't get slapped playing with me, Miyani? What the

hell is going on?" The moment the question left Dream's mouth, Gavin and Lexx walked in. Just like I knew they would.

"Givenchy called the wedding off," I spoke nonchalantly because I no longer cared. Internally I was hurt but tired of caring about the shit.

"Wait! Wait! There has to be some type of misunderstanding."

"No! There is no misunderstanding Gavin. We got into it, and I said some shit that wasn't cool. It angered him to the point where he physically yanked the ring from my finger and said the wedding off."

"What the hell did your bougie ass say that would piss him off like that?" Dream asked as she stared at me through narrowed eyes.

"Basically, he ruined my life. I didn't mean it. I love Givenchy. It's just that I've been through so much lately." Before I knew it, I had officially broken down in tears.

"Aye, step out! Let me talk to Miyani for a minute." All the air left my body, hearing Givenchy's voice. It dripped with anger. I couldn't even look up at him.

"We'll be right outside listening so keep ya damn hands to yourself."

Dream loves threatening these niggas like they won't fuck her up. I love how she rocks for us, though. She's that protective friend that every girl needs in her life.

The room was filled with awkward silence. The hairs on the back of my neck stood up, feeling his presence standing over me. His Sauvage cologne tickled my nose.

"Look at me, Miyani."

"I can't," I cried.

"Look at me right now! Wipe your eyes."

Givenchy walked around to my side of the desk and

kneeled in front of me. He wiped my tears with some Kleenex, and that only made me cry more.

"I'm sorry for what I said. I didn't mean it."

"Yes, you did. Look at me. When you speak on some shit, you have to stand ten toes behind it. That's how you feel, and I have no choice but to respect it. Listen to me, Miyani. I'm not upset with you because you said how you felt. I've always told you to be free with me. Honestly, you were right. Life for you has been fucked up since you got with a nigga. Sometimes the truth hurts. That's why I reacted the way that I did. By the way, I'm sorry for snatching the chain off your neck and taking the ring back. You didn't deserve that. I have a lot on my plate, and it needs to be handled. Some time apart will do both of us good."

"No, it won't do us good. We can't fix this if we're not together. Let's go home and deal with this. We both did and said things we didn't mean."

I jumped up from my seat and wrapped my arms around his neck so tight. It was a shame this man made me feel like a little girl in his presence. At this very moment, I needed him in every way. My heart and soul yearned for this man.

"The last thing I ever thought is that I would make life worse for you. Look at your fucking face! Them bitches sliced your shit because you love a nigga. That shit fucks me up every day! It's my fault you lost the baby. Them niggas made an example out of you because I came at them about being the mayor."

"Wait a minute! What are you talking about?" Givenchy had never ever let on that he knew who was actually behind my arrest.

"Let's just say that you're free because I made a deal to

not run for mayor. I didn't hesitate when the deal was placed on the table. I would give all this shit up if it meant that you would be out of jail. This why I'm so fucked up behind all this shit going on. I have a lot on my fucking plate, and I'm being pulled in all directions. Right now, I need you to understand it's better if you take the kids and go out of town for a while. Y'all don't need to be here with all this shit going on. I'm not risking y'all safety anymore. Tomorrow you and the kids will board a flight to Haiti. Chanel is expecting you."

My tears dried up fast, and anger consumed me. How he just gone come in here and say I'm going to Haiti?

"Nigga, you tripping! My life, our kids' lives, is here with you, not in no fucking Haiti. I suggest you get your money back. We're staying right here."

"Don't fight me on this, Miyani!"

"Look, I don't have shit out here in this world besides you and our kids. Do you actually think I'm about to go to Haiti and leave you here alone? Not only are you fighting your own battles, but you're also fighting mine too. Trust me. I brought trouble to your doorstep as well. So, I never should have made you feel like you made my life so bad, especially when you have made me the happiest woman in the world. Look at me, united we stand and divided we fall. These people who are out here trying to break us up will win if we fold right now.

After everything we've accomplished together, we can't let them win now. We cannot let Team Supreme down. You are the head of this family, and we don't fold around this motherfucker. I don't like this thing you're doing with me right now. The man I fell in love with never lets an enemy see him sweat. Chin up and chest the fuck out. I'll see you tonight when you get home."

I forcibly grabbed his face and roughly kissed his ass. Fuck all that crybaby shit. I needed to boss the fuck up and stand beside my man. All he has ever done was uplift me and make me feel better about myself. I decided to put him taking my ring back and ripping off my chain to the side. Right now, my man needed my support. The weight of the world was on his shoulders, and he needed me to do my part. I was no longer playing the back burner at Team Supreme. It was time for me to make my mark on this city.

TWO

GIVENCHY

A nigga had never been so overwhelmed with life, ever. Never did I think shit would have me about to lose my sanity. Shit with Miyani and me was all bad. It killed me to even think we might not be able to make it out of this bull- shit. Just knowing she felt like I fucked up her life hurts like a motherfucker. When I walked into her dance studio that day, all I wanted was to give her a life beyond her wildest dreams. At first, I was making all her dreams come true. The shit has quickly turned into a never-ending nightmare. Miyani is too good of a woman to be dealing with a nigga so deep in the streets like me. My family is involved in more shit than she knows. I've only allowed her access to certain shit. Now I'm just feeling like my thirst for power has ruined my life with Miyani.

Taking a long pull from my blunt, I looked at my invitation to the Bosses Roundtable. A nigga had finally secured his spot amongst the most elite of dope boys. Now that I have it, I'm not sure I want it anymore. I have too much unfinished business that needs to get handled. There was no way I could attend the Bosses Roundtable without handling my shit. It's the right thing to do. I just hope the nigga Thug don't take it as a sign of disrespect.

I placed the invitation back into the glove compartment before hopping out of the car. I had been sitting in my car outside of the house for about an hour.

Although Miyani and I had made up after our argument, we were keeping a distance from each other, but not in a negative way. It was more of us loving on each but giving each other some much-needed space. The shit was awkward as fuck, and I'm sure she felt the same way.

"Daddyy! I've been waiting for you to come in all night."

I didn't even get in the door good before Gianna and G-Baby came at me full speed ahead. My boy was walking and getting into everything. In a couple of months, he'll be two years old. It seems like Miyani just gave birth to him.

"What's up, lil nigga?" I dapped him up, and he took off in the opposite direction to Miyani. That little nigga fucks with his pops, but he's crazy about his Momma.

"Why have you been waiting for me?"

"You promised we would watch movies as a family tonight." I had forgotten all about it. The look on Miyani's face showed how disappointed she was.

"I'm sorry for being late. I'm here now. What are we going to watch?" As I spoke, I followed Miyani into the kitchen.

"I want to watch *Paid in Full*. It was messed up how he did Mitch in that hallway." She shook her head and walked out of the kitchen.

"You really need to make Ms. Gladys stop watching hood movies with her. Do you know she knows *New Jack City* word for word?" Miyani laughed.

"All black kids should know about the hood movies. It's

our culture. I'll make sure to talk to my granny, though. How was your day, beautiful?" I wrapped my arms around her waist and placed a passionate kiss on her lips.

"It was busy. I went for my last appointment before my surgery, and everything is ready. All my labs came back normal, and the surgery is set for next week. I'm nervous but ready to get this over with. I hate this damn scar. It makes me look so fucking ugly." Miyani smoothed out her hair to make sure it covered the scar. Just the thought of how the shit made her feel angered me.

"You're still the most beautiful girl in the world to a nigga. Nothing will ever change that." I couldn't wait for her to have the surgery so she can get her confidence back. It's hard complimenting her on her beauty when she no longer believes she's beautiful.

LATER THAT NIGHT, I laid in bed, contemplating my next move. Melissa and Butch were in the wind. The fact that the bitch could slither her way out of jail is beyond me. I can't wait to torture both of their ass behind all this bullshit. Not only did I have to get them, but I also needed to get at the governor, the state's attorney, and the fucking treasurer. All of them motherfuckers had a hand in Miyani being locked up. Once I handled them, I could move forward with my future plans for Team Supreme.

"Oh my god, G! You got your seat at the Roundtable. I'm so happy for you. Why didn't you tell me?" Miyani spoke as she looked at the invitation.

My ass had forgotten to remove it from the glove compartment. Of course, the first thing she did when she got in the car was start touching stuff. It's like she be looking for shit to be out of place. Either that or she just nosey as hell.

"I didn't tell you because right now is not a good time. Right now, the only thing I'm focused on is handling the motherfuckers who hurt you and my family. That and getting you to the hospital in time for your surgery."

I cut the volume on the radio up in an effort to end this conversation. That shit was the last thing on my mind. Miyani was more excited than I was, not that I wasn't. It's just that with everything going on, I can't embrace that shit.

"What do you mean now is not a good time? It's the perfect time to do this. You can't pass this up. Team Supreme has worked hard as hell for this shit. Fuck everything else, baby! You and your family need to be sitting at that table."

"I appreciate that, but now is not a good time. Please drop it, Miyani."

"But Givenchy," she whined.

"I said drop it," I gritted.

A nigga didn't mean to say it like that, but I needed her to drop the subject. She folded the invitation up and placed it back in the glove compartment. I turned the radio back on and continued to the hospital. She was getting ready to get put under anesthesia, and that's the only thing we needed to be worried about. I grabbed Miyani's hand and kissed the back of her hand. She needed to calm down because she was sitting in that passenger seat heated with a nigga.

That's another thing I need to get adjusted to. All of a sudden, she was quick to get angry. If I said something she didn't like, she would behave like a spoiled brat. Gone was the Miyani that allowed me to lead her. These days she wants to have a say so in everything. I'm all for freedom of speech. I want her to feel comfortable speaking her mind. At the same time, I'm still the head of the family. Whatever I say goes, especially when it has to do with Team Supreme. It's just certain lines I won't allow anyone to cross, not even Miyani.

THREE

MIYANI

It had been about a month since my surgery, and it had been a success. My face had healed perfectly. The Swedish doctor had worked his magic. It looked like I had never had a scar to begin with. For the last month, I had been resting and working from home. The walls of my house were closing in on me. My kids had spent the weekend with Ms. Gladys, and Givenchy was away on business, which sucked because I missed him so much. I was over being bored and home alone. Dream had given birth to a healthy baby boy. I hadn't been over to see the baby because I was healing. After grabbing the gifts, I had for the baby, I got ready to head over to Dream's house.

My car was being serviced, so I drove Givenchy's Wraith. When I got inside, I reach into the glove compartment for some wet wipes. I hated driving his cars because it always had ashes and weed all over the damn place. As I wiped up the residue. I took notice of the invitation to the Bosses Roundtable. His not RSVP'ing to the dinner had been bothering me. I know his ass still hasn't responded. After wiping things down, I sat staring at the invitation. That was when I came to the conclusion that I would RSVP for him. No matter what he said, I know this was what he wanted. Of course, he's going to be pissed, but he will thank me later. Yes, I'm fully aware that I'm overstepping my boundaries. At the same time, I won't sit back and watch him make a big mistake by not attending. The Alexander family deserves that seat at the table.

"STOP LAUGHING, BITCH!" Dream had been laughing at me all morning, and I was ready to fight her ass.

"I'm sorry, friend! You and G are funny as fuck. Why y'all so fucking dramatic? You crying cause the wedding off, and he's crying because he thinks he fucked ya life up. I bussed out laughing listening to you crazy motherfuckers. Both of y'all are sick in the head in love. No, on some real shit though, you handled that shit like a boss."

"In that moment, I had to shift the atmosphere. I felt like he was about to try to say we needed to part ways. There was no way I was about to stand there being no weak bitch. Plus, Givenchy is overwhelmed. All this shit going on has him stressed the fuck out. I'm really worried about him. Plus, that nigga was trying to send my kids and me to Haiti. I needed to do whatever because I wasn't going to no damn Haiti with Chanel."

I took a long pull on the blunt before handing it to Dream. Her ass had her son a couple of weeks ago, and she couldn't wait to start back blowing.

"We all almost lost it hearing him tell you that shit. I was gone be like Ms. Celie when Mister made Nettie leave on *The Color Purple*." We both fell out laughing. The shit she said was true because my ass would have been crying all while he dragged me to Haiti.

"So, how does it feel to be a mommy of two?"

"It's not as hard as I thought, but lately, I've been thinking about finding my birth mother."

Dream took a long pull from the blunt and stared out into space. This was always a touchy subject. The last time we discussed this, she was adamant that she would no longer try to find out where she came from.

"I'm with whatever you want to do. On the flip side, are you sure about this?"

"I'm very sure. Now that I'm a mother, I realize the importance of being a mom. I want to meet the woman who gave me life in the flesh. She needs to know that I'm doing just fine. I'm everything to my children that she wasn't to me. Not only that. I also want to know if I have siblings or any other family. Honestly, I walk around all day watching everyone around me spend time with their family. I know Fendi and his family accept me as one of their own, but it is not the same."

For the first time, I really saw emotion from Dream in regard to finding her family. She's always been so relaxed about the situation.

"You're more than just my best friend. You are my sister, Dream. I love you, and I'm here for you every step of the way. I've watched you go from being a bitch that didn't give a fuck to a woman who loves everything about this life. Your mother doesn't define who you are. I of all people know that."

"Yeah, but at least you were raised by Melissa's ass. That gives you leverage because you know the hoe is crazy, Miyani. I, on the other hand, don't know what I'm up against. What if she has Schizophrenia or some shit? I don't want my kids or me walking around with a gene we don't know about."

"What does Fendi think?" I just had to ask because he would never let her do this shit. He's protective as fuck over Dream.

"He told my ass not to go looking for skeletons that have the potential to hurt me."

"I'm sorry, but bro has a point." I had to keep it a buck with her.

"Who side are you on, hoe?"

"Yours, bitch! I don't want no smoke."

Although I knew she might not like what she finds. I'm going to support her through whatever. Lord knows she's been my strength when I didn't have it. It was only right I be the friend she needs on this journey.

AFTER A WEEK of being away on business, G had finally made it back. All week I had been anticipating his return. It had been a minute since we had any real alone time. As a matter of fact, it had been a minute since we actually had a good fuck session, not that we weren't fucking on a regular. It's just that we haven't been fucking like when we first met. That nigga needed to fuck me like he missed when he made it home. My ass was so horny I didn't know what to do.

My kids were spending the night with Versace, so it gave me room to really go all out. I had a personal chef come in and cook us a steak and lobster dinner. The shit looked so good I couldn't wait for him to come home and see everything that I had done.

I bit down on my bottom lip as I stood in front of my floor-length mirror. I was rocking a black, sheer one-piece lingerie from *Kurvie Krush*. By Michelle Necole. It was hugging every one of my curves too. A bitch looked so damn good I had to give myself a pat on the back. G-Baby knows he helped me gain weight in all the right places. At the same time, my ass didn't need to gain any more weight. I was no longer at a dancer's weight. All this good loving, fucking, and being spoiled had me being reckless. That added with being under so much stress. G had been keeping me in the house after I was released from jail. There was nothing for me to do but read, binge watch TV, and eat.

I'm so damn happy he let the reigns loose a little. A bitch raced getting out of the house and back to work full time. Going back to work really fucked up our personal time. That's why tonight had to be perfect.

Givenchy's flight had landed hours ago, and he should have been home by now. I had tried calling his phone, but it was going straight to voicemail. My ass started getting nervous. He was always so punctual when everything. This was out of the ordinary for him. My phone notified me that a text had come through. Quickly grabbing it, I realized it was a text from Dream.

BFF: *Bitch, I thought you were having a romantic night with G?*

Me: *I'm waiting for his ass now. His flight landed hours ago. I've been calling with no damn answer. Can you ask Fendi if he has heard from him?*

BFF: *Girl, them niggas up here at Club Bliss. Some big-time niggas bought the fucking club out. These a bunch of ignorant, wild motherfuckers too. I'm pissed cause this nigga Fendi purposely left me out of the loop. That's that sneaky dick shit I don't like. Put your shit on bitch and meet me up there.*

Me: *Nah.* *I'm good. I'll just wait until he comes home.*

As much as I wanted to go to the club and cut up, I didn't. That wasn't me. I never wanted to be that girl who made a scene in public with her nigga. Don't get me wrong. If it's warranted, I'll pop off wherever. I just feel like maybe the shit was important, so he had to attend the party. Plus, he's never made me feel like I needed to check on him like that. He still makes me feel like it's not a bitch out there that can compare. So, trust me, a bitch is not a worry of mine.

Despite that, I was heated because this nigga knew all about me wanting to spend some quality time. He didn't call me on purpose. Let me find out this how we carrying shit now. Lately, his vibe has been off. His nonchalant behavior was starting to rub me the wrong way. Now don't get me wrong. We've been good. It's just I miss the old carefree and loving Givenchy, not the uptight mean ass person he is now. All this bullshit and drama have stood in the way of our happily ever after. I don't give a fuck what's going on. I'm not about to let it ruin my fucking relationship. I've lost a lot behind it, but I won't lose him or our family.

<hr>

THE MOMENT I walked inside of Givenchy's section, he stood to his feet, which made the entire team stand in unison. It was if they all stopped what they were doing until I walked over to where G was standing. He grabbed me by the chin and placed a kiss on my lips. Sitting back down on the sofa, he poured himself a shot.

"What you doing here, beautiful? Sit down and relax."

"I was at home waiting for you. Now I know why you never made it. Why did you answer for me?"

"Some business came up, and it couldn't wait." He flamed up his blunt and took a long pull.

"Givenchy, you could have called."

"Sorry about that." He poured himself another shot and quickly knocked back.

Although the music was playing and the chatter around the club could be heard, the silence between us was louder. I grabbed the bottle of D'ussé and poured myself a shot. My ass needed a drink to calm me down. A bitch was seconds away to going straight the fuck off. This nonchalant shit is going to make me forget I love his ass.

Looking in the distance, I observed Dream and Fendi all hugged up. Dream talk a good tough ass game, but that nigga Fendi got her wrapped around his finger. We all know her ass will say different. I couldn't wait to talk about her ass. I wished I would have called Gavin or Lexx to meet us up here. At least I wouldn't be sitting here by my damn self. Givenchy continued to drink and engage in several conversations with different people. Trying my best, I chilled and watched him work the room without moving. People flocked to him like he was a king. No wonder his crazy ass wants to be mayor. These people feed his need for power. I must admit power looks good as fuck on him.

"Come sit on my lap, beautiful!" Givenchy licked his lips as I slid on his lap.

"I thought you forgot I was in the room," I spoke with an attitude as I adjusted my ass on his hard dick.

"I could never forget about you. I'm sorry for not calling earlier. A nigga's being pulled in all directions. Some shit came up that needed to be handled the moment I stepped off the plane. The shit's got me exhausted." He ran his hand over his face in frustration, and I truly felt bad. My ass needed to step up in a major way and help my man.

"I know that's why I was really expecting you to come home. A private chef came and cooked dinner for us. I had planned on riding that dick all night. The night was going to be all about you." I made sure to grind on his dick as I spoke.

"The night is young, beautiful. How about we head home and make this shit all about you?" Before I could even respond, about three officers stepped into the section. Givenchy was so quick on his feet he damn near knocked me off his lap. I quickly caught my balance and stood right beside him.

"What the fuck do you pigs want in my establishment? We legit. Baby, go get Menard on the line now!" Fendi was yelling.

"Calm down, Fendi. We're here for Givenchy."

"Here for him for what? He ain't did shit." My ass immediately started to go off.

"Calm down, baby." Givenchy quickly pulled me behind him. My heart was racing.

"Fuck y'all want with my brother!" Prada was up in the damn officer's face like he was crazy.

"Calm down. Y'all know we are only here doing our job. We have to arrest Givenchy for an aggravated assault on Nolan Banks." My eyes grew wide as saucers while looking at him. What the fuck did he do to my ex Noonie?

"Remember how I said shit was hectic from the moment I stepped off the plane?"

"Yes."

"Well, this is what I meant. Go home. I'll be there in a little while." Givenchy kissed me on the forehead and walked out of the section with the officers.

"That rat ass nigga deserved to get his fucking ass beat. I should have shot that bitch ass nigga in the fucking head!"

"Calm down, bro. You and Miyani go home. I'll check

on y'all in a little while." Fendi damn near pushed us out of the section.

Before I could make it home good, my phone was going off like crazy. Opening my IG, it was videos of Givenchy beating the shit out of Noonie. I cringed watching him break his legs with bats. What the fuck did Noonie do to make him do that? I thought all this bullshit with him was over. The nigga really brought this shit on himself. Despite that, I don't want Givenchy behind bars for his ass. The illiterate nigga is not worth it. This was some straight bullshit. I grabbed a bottle of wine and rolled me a fat ass blunt. It was about to be a long ass night. My ass was staying up until my man came through the damn door.

FOUR

GIVENCHY

As quick as the handcuffs were put on, they were taken off. I wasn't in jail an hour before I walked right back out. The nigga better be lucky I didn't kill his bitch ass. From the moment I stepped off the plane, the nigga was talking shit, all loud in the airport and shit. He started trying to flex, and the moment he spoke Miyani's name, I whooped that nigga ass. Prada pulled up in the midst of me beating his ass on the curbside. Without hesitation, he popped the trunk and handed me a steel bat. I started breaking every mother-fucking limb that I could. My goal was to end his fucking career behind that disrespectful shit. It had been months since he disrespected me reaching out to Miyani. The moment I see the fuck nigga, he got on that bullshit like I was a fuck nigga. So, I got on that gangsta shit with him. The preppy ass nigga didn't know what the fuck he had got himself into.

Walking in the house, I wasn't surprised that Miyani was wide awake. From the moment she came to live with me, she never fell asleep until I came home. I smiled as she stood and damn near jumped in my arms. That made a nigga feel good. I could only pray that once the smoke clears, she'll still be greeting a nigga like this.

"Ms. Gladys called and let me know that you were on the way home. I warmed you up some food in case you were hungry."

"A nigga's not even hungry. Come shower with me." I grabbed her hand and led her up the stairs to our bathroom.

"What happened with Noonie?" I should have known I wouldn't just be able to come here and not answer to her.

"Nothing you need to worry about and don't ever mention that nigga's name to me. Take that shit off!" I stepped out of my pants and quickly removed my shirt.

Miyani wasn't moving fast enough, so I ripped off the sheer nightie she on. After a long ass day of bullshit, I needed a release. Her pussy and her presence are the only thing to calm down the beast, brewing inside of me.

Stepping inside of the shower, I wasted no time lifting her. Backing her in the corner of the massive European styled shower, I went in. Miyani bit down on my shoulder as I pounded in and out of her. This wasn't some slow shit. This was straight fucking. See, I know what she needed to calm her ass down. Miyani morphed into a dick demon when I was deep inside of her. No matter how rough I got, she took that shit and fucked a nigga back with precision. We hadn't really been able to fuck and find time like we used to. So, a nigga had to go harder with the dick.

After fucking for hours, we laid in bed and smoked. I had zoned out and started thinking about our future. My ass had been working like a dog to find Melissa and Butch. I'm getting closer and closer. At first, I was growing impatient because I was ready to end this shit. Lately, I've been on chill mode because I know for a fact that sooner than anyone expects, I'll have a location on them. It's just a matter of time.

"Why do you love me, Givenchy?" That question took aback me because it came out of the blue. However, I'm glad she asked. Obviously, she needed to hear me speak that shit.

"I love you because with you is where I feel the safest. With you is what home feels like. I love you because you love me for me and not for who I am. I love that you're comfortable being yourself with me. You've never felt the need to go overboard to be someone you're not. That's real to a nigga like me. The most important thing that I love about you is I see a future with you. No woman has ever made me feel like she could have me for the rest of her life. You got the title and the bond, beautiful. Shit gets no better than that. Now tell me why you love me."

"I love you because you breathe life into me. You make me feel like I can conquer anything in this world. I love you because you pour into me on a daily basis. Every day I learn gems from you. I love you because you protect me at all costs. I've never been protected in my life. You are my savior in human form. I can't even imagine life without you and the kids in it. We've been through so much that we're about due for our happily ever after. I can feel it, Givenchy. The world is ours."

I sat in amazement, listening to Miyani tell me how she really felt. I would be lying if I said it didn't warm a nigga's heart to hear it.

"I want you to make me a promise, beautiful."

"Of course." She was too quick to say. After hearing my request, she might regret not thinking before answering the question.

"If I end up dead or in jail for the rest of my life, I want you to move on with your life. Don't sit and mourn over a nigga that's not coming back. Take the gems I taught you and fuck this city up. The same shit applies if I go to jail behind this shit. Don't wait for a nigga!"

Miyani quickly jumped out of bed and started going off.

"I don't want to hear this shit, Givenchy! Why are you saying this shit right now? Nothing is going to happen to you! Don't ever say no shit like that to me again! Do you hear me, Givenchy Alexander!"

"Calm down, Miyani."

"Don't tell me to calm down! The best way to make me nut up is the fear of losing you. I don't know how I'll survive if something happened to you. I'll probably die."

"If something happened to me, you couldn't die. You're stronger than that, and you have to be here to raise our kids. Come lay back down. I promise not to speak on it again. Remember, everything has your name on it. Shit won't move unless you say so. I didn't mean to upset you. In any case, you need to be prepared for whatever. Let me eat your pussy. That always calms you down."

Just like I knew she would, Miyani climbed in bed on all fours. She cums like a river when I eat that pussy from the back. The occasional dip of my tongue inside of her ass makes her cum back-to-back.

The sound of Miyani moaning and sniffling made me regret being so candid with her. I didn't know if my head game had her crying or the fact that she now thought something would happen to me. Either way, I wish I would have said nothing.

"WHAT'S GOOD, old lady? Why are you blowing my phone my up?" I asked as I walked into my granny's kitchen.

My stomach immediately growled, seeing her removing the first batch of chicken from the grease. Looking around, I realized that she had a whole feast going on. It wasn't a Sunday, so she was definitely up to something. Miyani and I had laid up fucking and talking all night, so a nigga was honestly still tired as fuck.

"It smells good than a motherfucker up in here!" Fendi said as he walked inside of the kitchen with Prada following close behind him.

"What the hell you up to Gladys? Since when you cook like this on a Thursday?" Prada spoke as he sat down at the table.

She still hadn't said shit to either of us. Instead, she grabbed a bottle of Wild Turkey and sat it in front of us. That could only mean the shit she was about to lay on us was heavy.

"I'm not drinking that shit! Last time you got me drunk off that shit, and I had a hangover for days. Give me that Rémy from the cabinet." I was not about to drink no damn Wild Turkey.

"Just get whatever the fuck y'all want to drink and sit down. I'm going to fix y'all a plate and get down to the real reason I called ya here."

"Here we go!" Fendi said, and we all sat down at the dining table.

Just like always, she placed a plate in front of each of us. Instead of fixing her a plate as well, she poured a double shot and joined us. I hurried up and started going in on the greens, baked macaroni, and fried chicken. With the way she was moving, I could tell she was about to tell me some shit that would ruin my appetite.

"Selena is back in Chicago."

"Who?" my brothers and I all said in unison. I damn near choked at the very thought of her being back in the city, especially since she had strict orders to never return.

"I got enough on my plate! I don't need this shit right now." I banged my fist on the table so hard I made the bottles of liquor fall over.

"I knew one day this shit would happen. That's why we should have killed her before she went back to Panama," Prada spoke up like I knew he would. The nigga loved reminding me of my fuckups.

"Selena is still like family. Now I don't agree with anyone killing her. She took a charge and did five years for the sake of this family. She never ratted on us or turned against this family. Y'all should actually be grateful. Let's at least give her the chance to explain why she's here."

Leave it to Gladys to try to be her Savior.

"There should be no reason why she's here. She had strict orders to never return. I have enough going on in my life right now. The last thing I need is Selena showing up and causing any type of drama."

I knocked back a shot and walked out of the kitchen. Hearing that shit had a nigga hot. She was given a nice severance package, so I'm lost as to what could have her back her. I haven't seen the bitch, and I want her gone already.

"You good, bro?" Fendi asked.

"Hell, nah! Selena should have her ass in Panama. I got rid of her ass for a reason."

"You still love Selena, huh?"

"I love Miyani. I don't feel shit for Selena. That shit is old as fuck. I appreciate her doing that time and not ratting. At the same time, she and I could never be shit again. I have a family now, so all that shit we used to do cannot ever happen again. Once all this shit clears, I'm marrying Miyani."

"I hear you talking, big bro. You don't have to convince me, but I do think you need to convince yourself. Selena has always been a badass bitch. Hell, I would be scared my dick was going to wander too. Just stay strong. I hate to be a pallbearer at your funeral. Miyani will definitely kill your black ass if you think about it." He laughed and walked back inside the house.

Selena Lacoste was a female that fucked with Team Supreme heavy. She used to do hits for us. She and I started fucking around right around the time India became pregnant with Gianna. India wasn't filling the void, and at that moment, Selena was fulfilling it. She did that shit a little too well because I started to neglect the fuck out of India. The shit had got so bad that I began flaunting Selena around town like she was my main bitch. I had to cut her off because India found out about us. I wasn't about to jeopardize my family for Selena. It was more so about my daughter. I couldn't risk losing her, so I got my shit together and welcomed family life. Even though I ended our relationship, I still allowed her to work for us. On one of the many gun runs, she was pulled over and arrested. Selena took the charge and never ratted the family out. I now know that it was India who ratted her out.

During her time away, I made sure she always had some shit on the books. It was from the entire family, letting her know we appreciated her. She got out about a year before I met Miyani. We sat her up nice in Panama, where her mother lived and gave her two million dollars. She had strict orders not to return. The last thing I need is someone added to the list of people who got it out for me. I don't give a fuck what my grandmother is talking about. If she moves funny in the least expected way, I'm going to murk her ass.

Selena was in her feelings when she came home. She was under the impression that we had a chance. At the time, the only thing on my mind was Team Supreme and my daughter. I didn't have any room or time for a woman. Not long after that, I met Miyani, and my feelings changed. I'm sure she feels some type of way about that. That's something she'll simply have to deal with on her own. I want no parts of the shit.

Looking at my watch, I realized that I was late for a meeting with my lawyer who also doubled as a private investigator. He had reached out and let me know that we needed to have a sit-down. I was surprised when he asked my grandmother to be in attendance. That request was quickly denied. I needed to hear what he had to tell us first before she even gets wind of it. If I had a chance to rectify it without sending her over the edge, that's what a nigga would do.

"WHY THE FUCK you got all of us here, Murray?" Fendi asked. Everybody was in attendance.

"Calm down. What I'm about to tell you all cannot leave this room. The information that I'm about to give you have not been run by the state's attorney just yet. The case is being built in the office, though, and I'm pretty sure she will give the go-ahead."

He slid folders across the conference table to all of us.

Without hesitation, we all opened them up at the same

time. I'm sure the lump that formed in my throat also formed in my brothers. The first page was titled *Operation Cage Team Supreme* with all our mugshots on the front. They even had Nettie up there, and she was no longer a part of the team. The shit has me shook looking at my granny mugshot. They were trying to take Ms. Gladys down too, and that would never happen.

"This some bullshit!" Prada spoke as he exhaled and sat back in his seat.

"Fuck they trying to do the team?" Butta asked.

"Give it to us straight, Murray. What these people on with us?" I asked sternly. He needed to lay that shit out there on the table.

"Team Supreme is set to be indicted in the next couple of months for several violations under the Rico Act. This is a new case being developed. It has nothing to do with the case that India was on. All that shit was thrown out. These are all new charges, and they're keeping it under wraps. This is not one of those situations where you get a slap on the wrist. They're even trying to get to the judges who aren't in your pockets. Trust me. This shit is about to get real. This is about as much as I know. As it comes to me, I'll pass it to you. Please talk to Gladys. She'll kick me off the payroll if she finds out I didn't come to her."

"Don't worry, Murray. Your position on the payroll is secured. Thanks for the information. We'll be in touch." We all dapped it up and left his office.

"So, what's the move?" Prada asked.

"We're not doing a day in jail. If they want to take us, they gone have to kill us. I don't know about you niggas, but I don't plan on dying anytime soon. We still have that place out in Atlanta. We can pack up the girls and stay out there on the estates if we have to. Right now, we have time. Let's chase this paper, make sure shit straight on all the properties, and shit secure for our families. Let's be proactive, so if shit gets real, we'll be good. Let's head over to headquarters and put this shit in motion. For now, we can keep Chanel and Gladys out of it. We can handle this on our own."

"No doubt, bro!" Fendi added.

"I'm not telling either of them shit. They be calling themselves getting rid of beefs, but be creating more beef in the process," Prada stated, and he was right.

Both were too damn busy for their own good. I loved them ladies, though. They would go to the end of the earth to keep us free and alive. Although Chanel left us and went back to Haiti to run shit, I had no choice but to respect her. She was a boss in every sense of the word. My OG was a force to be reckoned with. My granny taught her everything she knows, and they feed off each other's need to be powerful. That same need invokes me. A nigga like me wants all the power, and I will get it or die trying. These motherfuckers don't know who the fuck they're dealing with, but they'll soon find out.

FIVE

SUBSCRIBE

Working at Club Bliss had turned out to be one of the best decisions I had made. In such a short time, I've learned so much. I was so happy when Dream gave me the job to run things while she was on maternity leave, and I've done that shit like a boss, and I feel like I'm ready to venture out and start my own party promoting business. It was time for me to build my own empire now that Dream was off maternity leave. Since the moment I could walk, Chanel groomed me to get that money by any means necessary. If it were up to her, I would be back in Haiti helping her run my father's drug empire. I was groomed to take over in years to come. However, that's not my dream, and that's not the risk I want to take.

Coming to the United States was the best thing we could have ever did. Watching Dream, Miyani, and Gavin hold my brothers down made me want to boss all the way up.

All my life, I've had to live according to the way Chanel wanted me too. Of course, I know she means well. It's just I should never have let her talk me into marrying Joffery. Just because I was pregnant didn't mean I should have married him. At the same time, I know that it was more, so a business move on my father's behalf. My father is gone, and Joffery's family refuses to do business with my mother. She's been trying to get me to come back to Haiti for a sit-down, but I refuse to.

Chanel will not trick me into coming down there and dealing with Joffery ass. As a matter of fact, his ass is dead to me. My son is eight months old, and he has yet to show his ass up. I gave his ass an ultimatum, and he chose to stay in Haiti. One thing I won't do is force my son off on anyone. I may be young, but I'm no dummy. I can carry my own, and I don't need a nigga for shit, not when I got three big brothers that spoil my son and me rotten. Fuck Joffery, and I mean that shit from the bottom of my heart.

***

"THANKS FOR HELPING me with payroll. I owe your ass for this," Dream spoke as we placed payroll checks inside envelopes. Fendi was supposed to deposit the checks into the accounts but forgot. Now, we have to pass out paper checks to the employees.

"No problem. You know I'll do anything for you. Plus, I don't want to have to beat one of these bitches' asses about getting paid. That hoe Kim almost made me choke the shit out of her for popping slick."

"I had to send that bitch home about that shit. Fendi let these hoes get away with so much for so long. When I took over the day-to-day operations, I hired damn near a whole new staff. Kim is one of the original workers, so she thinks that she is exempt. I had to give that hoe a reality check. I run this shit here, and if you don't like it, take your ass home. This my first damn day back from maternity leave, and I'm ready to take my ass home. Fendi be pissing me off when he doesn't do his job. That shit always makes me have to do extra work. I don't know where I would be had I not hired you to help. I really appreciate this, sis."

"Stop thanking me. We're family. You've taught me so much. Plus, being here beats my grandma all in my damn business. I don't know who's worst her or my momma."

Both had been getting on my nerves. My momma wanted me back in Haiti, and my grandma keeps trying to hook me up with that crazy ass boy Dex. Ever since Butta been taking those trips for G, she's been hanging with Dex. I'll never understand why them niggas like hanging with that old ass lady.

"Ms. Gladys is not your typical old lady. She's a gangster granny that hangs with gangsters. Butta and Dex be out here on bullshit with her. Plus, they all gamblers, so they really fuck with each other hard."

"I don't know why they gamble with her ass. She be cheating. Her dice are loaded." Both Dream and I fell out laughing. Gladys was a real con artist. Since Chanel has been gone, I've become really close with her.

"I knew it. That's why I refuse to play poker with her ass. Here you pay the dancers. I'll go pay security and the bartenders."

I grabbed the checks and headed down the stairs to the dancer's locker room. On the way down the stairs, I ran into most of the girls working the floor. I handed them their paychecks and had one check left. Heading down the stairs, I stopped and observed my brother Prada. He was in a heated conversation with a dancer named Oni. My nosey ass quickly jumped back so that they wouldn't see me. I needed to hear what the fuck was being said.

"Stop talking to me, Prada! I'm over this shit. All you have to do is show up for the DNA test. I'm lost as to why you keep coming at me all aggressive and shit. Tiyonni is your daughter, and the DNA test will prove it." I covered my mouth in shock, listening to what she said. Gavin was going to kill my brother.

"Don't fucking play with me! Bitch, I paid for a fucking abortion. Now all of a sudden, you pop up talking about I have a three-year-old daughter. I should murk your ass for this bullshit!" Prada had pulled his gun out and placed it to the middle of her forehead.

"You know I love that kinky shit!"

"Don't try me, and you better not even think about playing with my girl behind this shit. I'll take the test, and when that shit comes back negative, stay the fuck away from me." He pushed her ass away from him, and all she did was laugh.

Prada walked off right pass the corner where I was hiding at. Without hesitation, I walked up on Oni quick.

"One thing I don't like is a liar. When I hired you last month, you acted as though you didn't know who owned this club. I see that's a lie. Listen to me and listen to me well. Do not play with my brother about a child being his. If your ass is lying, I'll beat your ass myself." I basically threw her ass the check and walked away in search of Prada.

I intended to curse him the fuck out, but that plan went out of the window when I saw Gavin come inside the club and greet him. His ass was lucky, but first thing tomorrow, I'm on his ass. I love the way she loves my brother, and she doesn't deserve to be hurt. He needs to tell her about this before I do.

AFTER A LONG ASS DAY, I decided just to head home. My ass was tired as fuck. All I want to do is take me a hot bath, sip some wine, and read a good ass book.

"What's up, bro? Dream is so pissed off."

"I know. She just cussed my ass out. I will make it up to her. Some shit came up that we had to handle. Thanks for coming in and helping her out. I owe you big time."

"You know I don't mind. I'm about to head home. This my weekend off but call me if you need me." Fendi and I exchanged a hug as I gathered my things.

As I walked out of the club, I bumped right smack into Dex.

"Damn! Big shoulder ass girl. Where you in a rush too?"

"None of your business." I rolled my eyes and walked right on past his ass.

"Your ugly ass always got an attitude!"

"Nigga, you got me fucked up! It ain't shit ugly about me. You got me mixed up with one of them ugly ass bitches you fuck with."

"I only fuck with bad bitches, love." He winked his eye and walked inside of the club. I wish I would have had a rock I would have thrown it and bussed his damn head.

Getting inside of my car, I hauled ass trying to get home. All I was thinking about was my bed. I immediately cut the ringer off on my phone because I didn't want to be bothered by anyone.

"VERSACE!" The sound of my grandma yelling my name made me sit straight up.

Her old ass would give someone a heart attack calling them like that. I'm knocked the fuck out, and she knows it. I swear I'm going my ass home tonight. You can get no sleep at Ms. Gladys' house.

She continued to call my name, so I got up and headed downstairs. I stopped in my tracks seeing Joffery holding my baby and about six of his men surrounding him. My grandma had a big ass shotgun aimed at them.

"Put the gun down, grandma. He's cool."

"I'm not putting shit down. He don't roll up to my motherfucking house with these big, black, crazy mother-fuckers! I hope they have this same energy when your brothers get here."

"No, really. Calm down, grandma. It's cool." This lady still had the shotgun pointed at Joffery while he had my baby.

"It's not cool. I don't know how the fuck they roll in Haiti. This is Chicago, and when niggas roll up on bitch deep like this, it means they want some smoke. Trust me. I got all the motherfucking smoke they want. The only question is who wants this hot shit first!"

"I'm sorry for coming to your home for my family. I meant no harm. Get dressed, Versace. I've come to get you and my son so that you can come home where you belong. Let's not forget our arrangement, or have you forgotten?

"As far as I'm concerned, our arrangement is null and void. You knew the circumstances of how I ended up here. When we spoke, you chose Haiti. That choice is the reason why we're done, and I'm staying here. I'm sorry you made the long ass trip for nothing." I walked over to him and took my son from his arms.

"You need to speak with your mother about the terms of our agreement. When your father passed, he didn't finish paying my family what was owed."

"Wait a minute! Why does she need to speak to

Chanel?" My grandma asked as she finally put the shotgun down.

"Chanel promised my family that if Versace had a boy, he would be raised by my family in Haiti. I'm here to take my son back home. As far as I'm concerned, you can stay here. I only requested that you leave with me so that you can at least see him once a week. I've taken on another wife, so your presence really doesn't matter at this point." My heart raced, and I felt light-headed hearing him say that.

"You not getting my baby. Now get the fuck out!" My voice cracked as tears flowed.

This shit had hit me. How could my mother offer up my son? She never discussed this with me, but shit was becoming so much clearer now. This is why she's been on my ass about me coming to Haiti.

"You heard what she said, nigga! Now you and the rest of your ugly ass crew can get the fuck out! If you even think about fucking with my granddaughter or grandson, I'll kill your ass with my bare hands."

My granny moved closer to Joffery, and he backed up in defeat. He winked his eye at me and walked out.

I sat on the couch and cuddled my son. All I could do was cry. My mother betrayed me.

"How could she do that?"

"Stop crying. Grandma is gone take care of everything. Let me call your brothers and get them over here, right now! That damn Chanel is forever on some bullshit. I should have known this shit was bigger than her just missing you and the baby. She has lost her mind if she thinks we would ever let that happen. Take him upstairs and bathe him. That old rough, raggedy, looking ass nigga got him smelling like Old Spice, and what the fuck is them things on top of his fucking head?"

"They're called wicks."

"That shit looks a hot ass mess. He got my pressure all the way the fuck up, coming up in my damn house with all that gold in his mouth and his hair standing on top of his damn head! I can't believe you laid down with his rough-looking ass."

"Actually, his gold teeth and wicks are what attracted me to him." She looked at me like I was crazy and walked off, talking more shit. If I weren't so hurt, I would have fallen out laughing at her.

"How could my momma go against me like this?" I spoke out loud as I begin to bathe my baby.

I needed to calm down and smoke a blunt before I called Chanel. After this conversation, we may not ever talk again. Either that, or we will be into it with each other. I guarantee I will forget she birthed me when I read her, her rights. Her ass is dead wrong for this shit and it has me looking at her differently. This is my son. I fought hard to bring him into the world safe and away from the bullshit. I'll fall out with anybody behind my son. My momma and Joffery are about to see a side of me they didn't know existed.

"CALL HER NUMBER AGAIN!" Givenchy had been standing over me going off for the last ten minutes.

"She's not answering for me." I was frustrated as fuck at Chanel. She had cut her phone off.

"Chanel's ass is dodging all of our fucking calls. She knows we know about the shit. I swear she needs to answer the fucking phone before I take a flight to Haiti," Fendi spoke as he paced back and forth in the living room.

"Prada was sitting on the couch, loading all these enormous ass guns. He and my grandma needed to calm down. She had on a damn army fatigue jogging suit with combat boots, not to mention the black makeup underneath her eyes like she was a damn soldier. This lady was war ready. I'm trying my best to sit here and not laugh at these crazy motherfuckers. I hope Joffery caught a flight back to Haiti because he was not ready for this crazy ass family of mine.

"I'm right with you. Her ass done lost her mind offering up my nephew. I don't care what excuse she has. Chanel ass is wrong. try to call her again, granny."

"I'm not calling that bitch no more, Prada! She has forty-eight hours to call us, or we're taking a flight."

"I have enough bullshit going on right now! Chanel's ass better reach out. I swear if we have to take a ride to Haiti, I might kill her myself. I'm pissed the fuck off because this nigga popped up here. How in the fuck does the nigga know where you were at anyway?"

G was fuming. I see why Miyani be on the verge of tears when they get into it. His old mean ass. He's been the main one hollering and yelling at my ass.

"I told him where I was at months ago. He has my address and granny's. I had no idea he would come, bro. He knew about us being here, and I gave him a choice. He could come here for his family or stay his ass in Haiti. Of course, he chose Haiti. Why he has shown up after all of this time is beyond me."

"Get dressed, Versace. I think it will be better if you stayed at the house with Miyani and me. I don't feel comfortable with you being home alone."

"Absolutely not! I'm not about to be all up in your space. You and sis need y'all time together. We will be fine."

"Well, make room for Dex," Fendi added.

"What do you mean make room for Dex?"

"That's what I mean. Since you don't want to get in the way at G house, then Dex will be staying with you until we get up with your bitch ass husband! This discussion is over, Versace. Fix your face. All that eye rolling got you looking ugly as fuck. I'll have Dex come over here and grab you."

"So, basically, I don't have a say so in this."

"No, the fuck you don't!" Prada said, and that made me even madder. I don't know who the fuck they think they are. Fendi knows that I hate Dex ass, so I believe he's doing the shit on purpose.

Instead of arguing with them, I just let the shit go. I had no win. It's all fun and games having big brothers until they in your fucking business. I needed to smoke me a fat ass blunt. The day's events have me stressed the fuck out.

"WHY WOULD you leave like that without telling me? Are you trying to have me into it with your brothers? Your ass knows damn well all you had to do was wake me up, and I would have taken you." Dex was talking and following me through the house.

"I needed some me time if you don't mind. You're with me every damn minute of the day." He had got on my last nerve. A bitch couldn't piss without him standing by the damn door. I was a minute away from losing my fucking mind.

"Trust me. I don't want to be around your bitter ass all day, either. However, I have a job to do, and I'm going to do it. Stop walking around this bitch acting like a spoiled ass brat. You have a big ass family that's worried about you and little man's safety. Your ass is ungrateful."

"Don't forget you work for me."

"I don't work for you. I'm doing a favor for your brothers because I fuck with them the long way. Do me a favor and let me know if you want to go somewhere?"

"Nah! You do me a favor. Keep your feet off my fucking coffee table, let the toilet seat down, and stop eating all my damn food!"

I slammed my bedroom door in his face and fell across my bed. My brothers called themselves keeping me safe, but all they were doing was making me miserable. Joffery hadn't reached out since he popped up. He's most likely went his ass back to Haiti. For his sake, I hope so.

As I laid across my bed, all I could think about was my mother. We still hadn't heard from her. For a minute, I thought maybe some shit happened to her. Then I remembered who the fuck I was talking about. Chanel's ass is fine. Knowing her, she's somewhere cooking up another scheme. That's a bag chasing ass lady, but at some point, she needs to stop taking risks.

The decisions she makes have had a profound effect on all her children. I just don't understand what it will take for her to stop taking these stupid ass chances. When I first found out about the deal she made, I was angry. Now I'm numb to it all. Her ignoring me and my brothers' calls speaks volumes. As far as I'm concerned, she can stay in Haiti away from me. I no longer want an explanation or an apology. Distance for her is all the hell I need.

SIX

DREAM

Hearing Fendi pull up to the house made me sit up in bed. It was five o'clock in the morning, and the sun was coming up. Yeah, this motherfucker had lost his mind. He knows I don't play these types of games. I don't give a fuck about a nigga being out handling street business. My problem is with a nigga that likes to hang out and get fucked up. I don't give a fuck that he owns Club Bliss. He doesn't need to be there all night partying like he's not a fucking boss. The shit is not a good look.

"I know, baby. Gone head and curse me out," he slurred as he stumbled through the front door. He barely made it to the couch without bussing his ass.

All I could do was look at him and shake my head. From the moment we got together, I knew he liked to hang out so, barriers were established. Within the last month, he's been back to his old ways.

"I'm not about to say shit to you while you're drunk as fuck, but please believe that when you sober up, I'm going to get on your ass!"

"I'll slap the fuck outta you! You know I don't play them stupid ass games." He tried to sit up, but his drunk ass fell right back over.

I cringed, thinking that this nigga was going to vomit on my damn sofa. I pray his ass woke up with a hangover from hell in the morning.

After setting the alarm, I headed back upstairs. Exhausted wasn't the word. Between sitting up worrying about Fendi, I had been dealing with a cranky baby. He had finally gone to sleep, and I was about to get some much-needed rest with him. My daughter was with Miyani, so that was a big help. It's been a struggle to try to run the business, tend to my wifely duties, and be the ultimate mother to my kids. I want to complain about the heavy load I'm carrying, but I wouldn't dare. God has blessed with the one thing I've prayed for all my life — a family of my own.

"SO, you just gone walk around all day and not talk to a nigga?" he asked as he placed kisses on the side of my neck.

"Move Fendi. I'm trying to do my makeup."

I had been ignoring his ass all day. He basically slept the day away. Now he's up getting dressed, getting ready to hit the damn streets again. All day I had been thinking about what I was going to say to his ass. Then I thought about it. Instead of me cussing at his ass out, I decided to pull a him on him. I needed me a day out of this fucking house. Ms. Gladys had all the grandkids for the night. Gavin, Miyani, and I decided to go out and kick it. It had been a minute since we had a night out on the town, so the shit was much needed.

"Since when you start pushing a nigga off you?" Fendi reached in between my legs and pulled my thong to the side.

"No! You're going to make me late." I managed to get out as he ran his fingers across my clit. The feeling of his dick pressed up against my ass made me loosen up. He hadn't even penetrated me, and the shit felt good.

"I'm sorry for coming home fucked up."

Fendi had bent down and placed soft kisses on my ass cheeks. My knees became wobbly as he spread my ass apart. Chills ran through my body as he swiped his tongue up and down my ass crack. A bitch had to grip the sink as he started to eat my ass from the back. This nigga knew I was mad at him, so he used his secret weapon against me. All logic goes out of the window when he starts eating my pussy.

I didn't want to come quick, so I turned around and lifted myself onto my vanity. Fendi stood to his feet and dropped his joggers. I bit down on my lip as I started to jack his dick.

He placed his hand on the mirror behind me to catch his balance.

"Make that dick skeet for me!" I seductively spoke as he skeeted all over my hand. That was just the adrenaline rush he needed to hop off in this pussy. Without hesitation, he had my ass spread eagle on the vanity fucking the shit out of me.

"Fuckkkkkk!" I screamed out, trying my best not to cum. He wasn't making the shit any easy as he fucked me into submission.

"You still mad at nigga?" Fendi asked as he sexily bit down on his bottom lip, all the while drilling dip inside of my pussy. If I was mad before, my dick silly ass wasn't mad anymore. He had fucked the mad right up out my ass.

"Noooo! Baby, I'm not mad anymore."

"Then cum on this dick." He began to vigorously rub his thumb across my clit while fucking me at the same time. Moments later, I was squirting all over the place.

"Ahhhhh, shitttt!" I had to wrap my arms around his neck and ride the waves of ecstasy as we came together. If I weren't on the Depo shot, a bitch would for sure get be pregnant again.

After that fuck, all I wanted to do was climb in bed and take my ass to sleep. That was until Fendi hopped in the shower and started getting dressed. What he thought was he was going to fuck me into staying home while he hit the streets. I don't fucking think so. I'm out the door right with him.

"I'M SO DAMN happy y'all invited me," Lexx said as she sipped from her glass.

"We all needed a damn break from the kids and them niggas. Fendi has called my ass twenty times trying to see when I'm coming home. His black ass got a lot of nerve checking up on me. His ass has been coming home late as fuck. His ass had better hope I don't let the sun beat me home."

I danced in my seat as we kicked it at Paradise. Lexx, Miyani, Gavin, and I had grabbed a section after dinner. We were two D'ussé bottles in and was nowhere near ready to head home. It was after one in the morning and we're partying are asses off. This shit had me missing the good ole days when I partied all night and slept all day. Fendi swooped his big dick ass in and cut that shit quick.

"Quit capping! Bitch, you know your ass not about to let the sun beat you home!" Miyani stated.

"I'll be leaving soon. The last thing I need is to be beefing with Prada. We are finally in a better place, and I want it to stay that way."

"Gunna's ass already mad I'm out kicking it. A bitch is not trying to go to the crib until he makes it in too drunk to give a fuck."

"I'm saying though. Why you think I'm capping? You know motherfucking well that I'll pull it and worry about the consequences later. Bitch, you be the one around here capping like you gone stand up to G. That nigga gets his way every time. He canceled the wedding, and you found a way to see the good in that shit!"

Fuck! I thought to myself the moment I saw the hurt on her face.

"Not cool. drunk bitch!" Gavin said as she snatched the D'ussé bottle from my hand.

"I didn't mean it the way it came out. At the same time,

you know I'm telling the truth. Givenchy gets his way, and you know it."

"You meant it, Dream. Don't worry about Givenchy and me. Worry about that toxic ass relationship your ass is in with Fendi."

"All that is not necessary. I'm not walking around here acting like my relationship isn't toxic. You, on the other hand, is trying to walk around like yours isn't. We all fuck with a gang of dysfunctional trigger-happy ass niggas. I said I didn't mean it that way, but you came for my nigga. I'll be sure to tell him how you really feel."

"You bitches are going too far tonight. That dark liquor got y'all doing the most. This is why we need to just stick to wine," Gavin added.

"I swear. You hoes need to kiss and make up right now," Lexx said, but before either of us could say anything, this nigga Noonie appeared out of nowhere.

"Let me talk to you, Miyani!" he slurred, obviously drunk.

"If you don't get your drunk ass away from here, nigga!" I gritted. He made my fucking skin crawl. It was something about him that I never fucking liked. The fact that he keeps popping up from time to time bothers the fuck out of me.

"I'm convinced you like getting your ass beat. I should be the last person you want to say anything to. Please move around, Noonie. Let this shit go!"

"Ya bitch ass nigga may have ended my career!"

"Serves your ass right for being on bullshit. You were warned several times to stop trying to get in contact with my sister. Don't bring your dumb ass over here with that bullshit!"

"That nigga's gone pay for what the fuck he did!"

Noonie acted like he wanted to do something, but that tone changed real quick. G, Fendi, Prada, and Gunna had popped up on our ass.

"Is that a threat, my nigga!" Givenchy had his gun pressed underneath Noonie's chin. He was for sure to piss on himself at any moment.

"Don't bitch up now. Talk that shit you were just talking!" Prada added.

"Put the gun down, Givenchy!" Miyani cried.

"Nah, sis! This nigga was over here talking too fucking disrespectful. He needs to just go ahead and put a bullet in his fucking head!" Fendi gritted.

My pussy was getting wet, watching him in action.

"Go home, beautiful. I'll see you when I get there." He winked his eye at her and focused right back on Noonie.

"No! I'm not leaving. Let's go now!" I could tell he was getting angry. In a minute, shit was going to go left. Come on! Let's go. I practically pulled Miyani out of the section. Gavin and Lexx were right behind us. Before we fully made it to the exit, you could hear them beating the fuck out of Noonie. If his career wasn't over at first, it most definitely is now.

IT HAD BEEN a week since the incident when we went out. Miyani and I still hadn't spoken to each other. I had called her several times, but the bitch wasn't answering for me. She was being so petty right now. Yes, I said some foul shit to her, but she disrespected my relationship as well by calling it toxic. I didn't take it personal at all. Why she's all in her feelings about what I said to her, I'll never understand. She might as well get ready because I'm going to pull up on her ass.

"How long will you be gone?" I was so sad because Fendi was going on a business trip out to Atlanta. With so much going on, I hated for him to leave. My nerves would be so bad until he comes back.

"Only for two days. I'll be back before you know it."

He grabbed our son from my arms and placed a kiss on his forehead. He loves our daughter, but he is crazy about his firstborn son. I have to remind him that he's a damn newborn because he keeps getting him jewelry pieces made. The shit weighs more than the damn baby.

"When you get back, I need to talk to you about something."

"Nah! Let's talk now. I'm not going to be able to focus on business thinking about what you have to tell me." I played with my fingers nervously before speaking.

"I recently met up with my old DCFS caseworker. She gave me some information about my birth mother. I'm going to follow up with it and see what I can find."

His jaw tightened because he hated it when I looked for my mother. He felt like all I need is him and our little family, which is true. All I need in this life was my man and our kids. However, I need to know what family I come from.

"I'm not going to say not to because that would be selfish of me. At the same time, I don't want anybody hurting you. You have to be prepared for some hurt behind this shit. Of course, I'll be right here. Promise me you won't let it get you down."

Tears welled up in my eyes hearing him speak so passionately to me. Fendi is real hardcore with his deliveries, so seeing this side of him warms my heart.

"I promise." We kissed each other passionately as he placed Baby Fendi in my arms.

"For what it's worth, I pray that you find some peace with this shit. I'll call you when we land."

He placed a kiss on both our son and sleeping daughter's forehead before walking out of the room. I really thought he was going to go off on my ass, but he didn't. Fendi must have grown tired with me talking about it.

I had been staring at the envelope for the longest but couldn't bring myself up to open it. Miyani promised she would help me do this, and now she's ignoring me.

Fuck this shit! I thought to myself as I got dressed to head over to her house. We're about to kiss and makeup whether she likes it or not.

"WHY THE FUCK are you banging on my door like that?" Miyani asked as she snatched her front door open. I politely pushed passed her and walked in her shit.

"Because you won't answer the fucking phone for me, bitch!"

"I have my phone cut off. What you want, Dream?" Her stank ass attitude had me pissed, and I didn't come over here to escalate the situation.

"Are you serious right now, Miyani? I can't believe your ass is still mad at me. You said something that was fucked up too, and I'm not walking around mad at you for it. This ain't even how we roll. What the fuck is good with you? Let me know now, and I'll move accordingly, going forward."

"I'm not mad at you, okay. I just needed some time for myself." Miyani plopped down on the couch and poured herself a shot of Patrón. She knocked it back like a stressed-out person. In that moment, I knew something was wrong with her.

"What's wrong? Where are the kids?" I sat across from her and poured me a shot.

"They're with Ms. Gladys."

"Okay. What the fuck is wrong with you?"

"Givenchy is cheating on me."

"Miyani, stop! That man loves you, and you know it. He would never cheat on you. Now Fendi is a pussy hound, so I wouldn't be surprised if he dipped on me. He also knows I'll cut his dick off and mail it to Ms. Gladys for playing with me. That's not how G moves. Why would you think he's cheating on you?"

"I saw him with her the day after the shit happened at the club. I wanted us to go out to dinner and spend some time together. He told me that he had to make a move with Fendi and Prada. I decided just to go out and grab something to eat at Fogo De Chao. He didn't even see me as I sat in the corner observing them. She was emotional and kept reaching across the table to grab his hands. Dream, they knew each other. She wasn't some random ass bitch. I could feel it in my heart. If she were a nobody, he would have told me. That's how I know something is up."

Miyani wiped the tears that had fallen. I quickly changed my seat and sat next to her. My friend was so damn dramatic. I wanted to buss out laughing at her, but she was already mad at me.

"Aww, friend! It has to be some type of explanation. I just don't see him blatantly cheating out in the open like that. You know that G goes out of his way to protect you. Just give him the benefit of the doubt. Did you at least say something about it?"

"No! There is so much going on in my head. I don't know where to start. Besides that, I've found Butch and Melissa whereabouts."

"Wait a minute. You found out where they are? Please tell me you at least told that man that?" I had to pour myself another shot to calm my nerves. Miyani had my pressure up with these revelations.

"No! I didn't tell him that either. If I tell him, then he will go and kill them. I just feel like I need that closure after everything that she has done to me. Butch is my biological father and has never stood up. Therefore, both of them owe me an explanation before I murder them."

"So, let's go. Let's confront them right now. You know I'm down."

"I just need to keep eyes on them a little longer. Don't worry. I have someone watching them bitches twenty-four/seven for me. They're not getting away this time. That hoe will pay for slashing me in my face."

I smiled, looking at my best friend. That hoe Melissa had finally brought the beast up out of Miyani.

"Please don't get at that hoe without me."

"I'm taking you and Gavin with me anyway. Now, why the hell are you over here?"

"Never mind all that. When you gone tell G that you saw him with that bitch?" That shit needed to be addressed immediately if it had her all in her feelings like this.

"When he gets back from out of town, I guess."

"Make sure you address that shit and not a minute after. Don't sit in here driving yourself crazy over nothing. Givenchy would never cheat on you, and I'll bet my bank account on that."

"You vouching for him big time, huh?"

"Hell yeah! That man loves your dirty draws. I watched

him shed tears behind you getting locked up and hurt. That man walked away from a dream he had to save you. Whoever that hoe is means nothing to him. Trust me. If that hoe was crying, he was letting her down gently."

I may sound crazy, but it's the damn truth. Givenchy loves the fuck out of Miyani. He wouldn't cheat on her. Givenchy Alexander is the type of man that will lay it all out there on the table, then give you the option of how you want to proceed.

"Maybe you're right. He hasn't changed up his routine or anything. I just hate that he lied to me. That's the part that's driving me crazy. If it were an innocent dinner, he could have told me that. I would have understood."

"Stop lying! No, the fuck you wouldn't!"

"You're right. I wouldn't! He still could have told me, though. Let's talk about something else. I need to get my mind off this shit before I drive myself crazy. As a matter of fact, I'm going to leave it alone all together for right now. Forget that I said anything about the shit. Let's change the subject. What's been going on with you?"

"I have an address on my birth mother."

"Oh my god! I'm so happy for you. Did you check it out?" Miyani was so damn excited as she wrapped her arms around me.

"I was too scared to just pop up over there alone. Honestly, that's why I'm over here now. You promised to be there with me on this journey. I'm usually tough as fuck, but this shit here is crazy. I can't go there by myself."

"I'm about to get dressed, and we're going to that address. Since the first day, we met you wanted to find out where you came from, so here is your chance." Miyani and I exchanged hugs before she took off up the stairs.

My ass was nervous about going to the address, but the shit needed to be done.

"THIS WAS A BAD IDEA. Let's just turn around." I was so damn nervous as Miyani and I headed to the address. We were about five minutes away, and my anxiety was starting to get the best of me.

"I know your big mouth ass is not chickening out. Not big badass Dream Brooks."

"It's hard to believe right. Hell, I'm shocked at myself. What if I knock on the door, and she slams it in my face? I mean, she did give me away for a reason."

"If she slams that door in your face, then that's the closure you need. You have a man and two beautiful kids that love you, not to mention a friend that will kill a brick and a building for you. If you want to turn around, we can."

Just hearing Miyani's calming voice gave me the courage I needed to follow through with this shit.

"I'm not going to turn around, but if that bitch pop slick, I'm beating her ass. She needs her ass beat for abandoning me. Had she kept me I never would have had such a fucked up life before meeting Ms. Charlotte. What could be so bad about life that it would make you give up your child?" Just the thought of being abandoned still doesn't sit right with me. I have everything a woman could want at home but not having any family makes me null and void.

For the next couple of minutes, I remained quiet as I got closer to the address. When we pulled up, the house looked old and raggedy, not to mention it was in the heart of the hood.

"I'm glad I have my gun in my purse cause this neighborhood don't look safe."

"Who you telling? Bring your bougie ass on. Let's get this shit over with," I spoke as I hopped out of the car.

My nerves were now replaced with adrenaline. A bitch had to know if my mother or anybody she knew lived at this address. Miyani grabbed my hand tight as we made it up to the door. Before knocking, I let out a deep breath and released all my anxiety.

"Can I help you?" A light-skinned older woman asked as she leaned up against the door frame. Both Miyani and me took a step back as she blew cigarette smoke in our direction. I became nervous as she looked at us, obviously upset we had knocked.

"My name is Dream, and I'm looking for Ginger Marshall."

"I'm Ginger. Why the fuck are you looking for me?" She stepped closer to us as she flicked the cigarette by our feet.

My heart raced, hearing her say that she was Ginger. I always wondered what my mother looked like. The lady standing before me looked like she was beautiful back in the day, but life hadn't been kind to her. Giving her a once over, I took notice of the ankle bracelet she had on. This damn lady was on house arrest. Why am I not surprised that I came from a damn criminal? Miyani squeezed my hand feeling me start to shake as I spoke.

"My name is Dream Brooks, and I'm your daughter."

All the life drained from her face. I could tell that she wanted to cry, but her tough demeanor wouldn't allow the tears to fall. I handed her the file, and her eyes showed it all. I was indeed then damn daughter she had given up. She was staring at her signature, terminating her rights to me.

"Why did you come look for me, Dream Doll? People give babies away for a reason. I wasn't fit to be a mother then, and I'm definitely not fit to be one now. From the looks of it, you've done well for yourself. You don't need me in your life creating chaos. Everywhere I go, trouble follows." She quickly tried to go inside and close the door. She wasn't quick enough because I promptly grabbed her in her collar.

"That's a poor ass excuse! I didn't come over here to hear excuses. You should have thought about that when you were out here fucking. Look at these two kids. Their names are Chanel and Fendi Jr. I gave them life. I'll always put them first no matter how fucked up my life becomes. I didn't know the first thing about being a mother when I found out I was pregnant with my daughter. When I laid eyes on her for the first time, I knew I would move mountains for her. Don't talk to me about not being able to be a fucking mother because of chaos.

Because you couldn't be a mother, I was passed around foster homes all my young life. I've been molested and raped so many times I started thinking that shit was normal. No matter what happened to me in my life, I've done what I had to do as a mother. Keep your excuses and clean your fucking self up. You too damn old to have on a fucking ankle monitor!"

She had me so angry that I went to choke the fuck out of her ass.

"Calm down, Dream!" Miyani said as she quickly grabbed me.

"What the hell going on, ma?" Both Miyani and me turned around and locked eyes with Dex.

"Is this your mother, Dex?" Miyani asked, shocked.

I was too speechless to even speak. Even though we

both heard him call her "ma", we were both trying to make sure we heard him right.

"Yes. Y'all good. Is something wrong?"

"Oh my god! No. nothing is wrong. I can't believe this shit right now." I had to hold on to the railing just to find some balance. I felt like my legs would give out. A link to who I am had been around me all the time.

"Would somebody tell me what the fuck is really good?"

"This is your sister. I terminated my parental rights and handed her over to the state. Back then, I just didn't have the means to take care of her. I'm sorry I did it, and I'm sorry I didn't tell you. I've been too far from the GPS box. It's beeping." She rushed inside the house, and I didn't even bother going after her.

Fuck that weak ass bitch. I didn't even care about who she was anymore. My heart felt so good knowing that Dex was my brother. The crazy part is that we always share inside jokes and shit when he helps at the club.

"You sure you didn't know I was your sister?" I asked skeptically because this shit was playing out like a Lifetime movie. The last thing my man needed was someone pretending to be down with his cause with ulterior motives.

"I had no idea. My OG has been fucked up since I've been in this world. Consider yourself lucky, Dream. You didn't miss out on shit. Do Fendi and Givenchy know y'all out here in the hood like this, with no security or shit?

"Fuck all that, Dex! You and Dream are sister and brother." Miyani old soft ass was crying, and that shit made me tear up.

"Looks that way, huh? Let me get y'all home before one of these niggas rob your ass for that Bentley. Then I'll have to burn this whole city down. A nigga can't be letting nobody fuck with his big sister."

Dex wrapped his arm around my shoulders, and it had a real bitch in tears. I woke up this morning, unsure of what the day would bring. Never in a million years did I think I would meet my deadbeat ass birth mother. That didn't go too well, and that's okay. Finding out that Dex was my younger brother was all the closure I needed. Fendi wasn't going to believe that shit.

SEVEN

DEXTER

I had been sitting outside of my OG house for the last hour. A nigga was too damn mad at my momma's ass. She could have told me that she had a child she gave up for adoption. Honestly, I wish she would have just given my ass up for adoption. Maybe I wouldn't be so fucking deep in the streets. I've been fending for myself since a little nigga.

Ginger didn't give a fuck. Her only concern was getting high. That's how it was then, and that's how it is now.

I just can't get Dream's face out of my head when she learned I was her brother. At twenty years old, I have no idea what it feels like to have a family. That's most likely why I've gravitated to the streets and Team Supreme. It's crazy how life can sometimes be. Fendi has been grooming me since I was twelve. Who would have known the connection we would have in years to come?

I've always loved to be around Ms. Gladys. She crazy as hell, but I learned a lot from her and Team Supreme growing up. I don't know where I would be had Fendi not took me under his wing. Every gem the man has ever dropped on me, I used that shit to elevate myself in the drug game. At twenty, I'm one of the youngest cats in the Chi running a whole stretch of the city for the Team Supreme. Life is so good, and just knowing that I have a sister makes the shit even better.

My phone rang, and I quickly silenced it. Versace was calling me for like the hundredth time. I already know she's mad cause I told Fendi on her stanking ass. They need to hurry and come back from out of town. On the one hand, I want to murder her, and on the other, I want to murder that pussy. Versace has no idea what the fuck she does to a nigga. I've been praying her bitch ass husband comes around so that I can murk his ass. Hell, I'm ready to be a shoulder she can cry on and a dick to ride on too. That is if I don't shoot her as first. Her mouth so fucking smart she'll make a nigga kill her ass and worry about the consequences later.

After facing a blunt, I headed inside the house. Dealing with my mother is so frustrating. That's why I stay the fuck away from her. The only reason I came over was to give her money for the month. I don't deal with her on a personal

level. We don't have that type of mother and son relationship most niggas have. I make sure she always has money for
her basic needs. What she does with it after I give it to her is
her business. Ginger is going to do what the fuck she wants
to do. The sad part about all of this is not even her daughter
showing up will change her.

"Don't come in here questioning me about shit!"

"I'm not coming in here to ask you shit. Obviously, you
didn't want me to know. Are there any more kids out there
somewhere?" I threw the money on the table, and she
quickly grabbed it.

"Not today Dexter. I'm not in the mood for this shit.
These damn people need to come and cut this fucking band
off my fucking ankle. They've been coming for two days
and still hasn't shown up. I need to make some fucking
moves."

"You mean, go get high."

Her nervous and jittery behavior was a visible sign she
was feigning for that shit. It used to break my heart to see
my momma this way. The shit doesn't even faze me
anymore. I'm honestly waiting to get the call that her ass
overdosed and died. Either that or back in jail doing a bid
for all the damn scamming she be on.

"Really, Dexter?"

"Hell yeah! I know your ass like a book. The sad part
about looking at you right now is that you hold no emotion.
The daughter you gave up for adoption just turned up on
your doorstep. Did it ever occur to you that maybe she
needed you? During the time that she stood on that fucking
porch, you held no emotion. Not once did you embrace her.
I'm not surprised, though. You don't know shit about being a
mother or expressing love to your seeds. In all my twenty
years, I've never heard you say that you love me. Come to

think of it, you've never made me feel like I was loved as a little nigga. Finding out that you have walked around like you didn't abandon your own daughter sickens me."

"Why the fuck does it sicken you? It was before you were ever born. You don't know what I went through back then."

"I don't care about what you went through. All I know is that all my life, you made me feel like I was a burden, and now I know why. You never wanted to be a mother. I'm just glad to know that Dream is my sister. She is so smart and hardworking. She is running multi-million-dollar businesses for the Alexander family. Clean yourself up and try to be a mother before it's too late."

I didn't wait for her to say anything. Her words weren't needed. She needed to show some fucking action. Until then, she was cut off, and I'm not fucking with her period.

I HAD BEEN SITTING in the VIP area of Club Bliss watching Versace. She was working the room, making sure everything was going according to plan. It was her first solo event, and after this shit, I'm sure the whole city will be booking events with her. It's crazy to see a young female on her shit. I admire the fuck out of her smart mouth ass. Her family is monied the fuck up, and she doesn't act like it. She liked to make her own money, and I admired that shit about her. I had to adjust my dick and get the nasty thoughts out of my head. Versace Alexander was off-limits. Givenchy, Prada, and Fendi all had a sit-down with me and made that shit clear.

"She's amazing, huh?" Dream said as she sipped from her champagne glass.

"Amazing with a smart ass mouth. That girl ain't shit but a jail or death sentence for a nigga. Versace is what a nigga would call forbidden fruit." I knocked back my shot and again focused on Versace.

"She's a wild girl. She kind of reminds me of myself when I was her age. She's so eager to learn and get to her next dollar. I admire her because she wants to be legit. Back then, all I wanted to do was look cute, shop, and hustle niggas out of their bread. Now I'm running corporations and cutting business deals. I never knew my life would turn out so good. I'm about to get married, I have two beautiful children, and now I have a brother." Dream's voice cracked, and when I looked over at her, she was shedding tears.

"Come on now. Don't do all that. There is no need to be sad about where you come from anymore. We're together now. There are still so many unanswered questions from Ginger. We have to let go asking why and just embrace this new life."

She was smiling from ear-to-ear as she fixed the collar of my shirt. It had been about a week since we found out we were related, and Dream had been acting like we knew each other our whole lives. The shit felt good but weird at the same time. Hell, the whole damn family was treating me differently. I liked it better when I was just a part of the team.

"I wanted to give you something." Dream handed me an envelope. Opening it, I realized it was a deed to a house.

"I have my own house already, sis. Even if I didn't, I wouldn't accept a dime from you. A nigga is just happy to have you as a sister."

"I know that. That's why it's not for you. It's for Ginger, fully paid for and in her name. All she has to do is get clean and stay out of trouble. It's all hers with no strings attached.

I no longer feel the need to press her about anything. Meeting her for the first time gave me so much clarity. It helped me to close that chapter and begin a new chapter. I have a little brother, and that's all the closure I need."

"You don't owe Ginger shit. She inherited that house from her grandmother and ran it right down into the ground. Ginger is a fuck up and always will be. She'll fuck around and lose this house to a drug dealer or some shit."

I hated that Dream was spending her hard-earned money on Ginger's ass. This gesture alone lets me know she's cut differently. Ginger gave her up for adoption, and here she is buying her house.

"No, she won't. I have a feeling that Ginger is going to get her shit together. Trust me." She winked her eye at me and walked off.

All I could do was shake my head because there was no telling what she was hinting at. I decided to leave it alone. I've been around Fendi enough to know that she's crazy than a motherfucker. I'll let her deal with Ginger her way and stay out of it. Maybe this gesture would help Ginger get her shit together.

Lately, I've just been sitting back, reflecting on my life and how successful my family is. The greatest feeling in the world to a nigga is knowing your seeds are straight for the rest of their lives. That's a different type of high. Just knowing that Dream was the mother of my children made the shit even better. I still can't believe I have a namesake to carry on my legacy.

Besides being content with family life, I'm happy for my wife. She's found the missing link to her life. Dex is good nigga and loyal as fuck. I have no worries about him when it comes to Dream. Now Ginger is another story. I don't trust her with Dream's heart period. I've watched my baby struggle with where she comes from. Just knowing that Ginger gave birth to her fucks with me.

Ginger is grimy as fuck, and I watched how she was never a mother to Dex. At twelve, he was on the block hustling to pay all the bills in the house. We loved the way the lil nigga moved, so we welcomed him into the family. Over the years, I've watched him evolve into a young rich nigga. During that time, I've watched him try to keep Ginger straight, but she refuses to. Now that she is aware that Dream is her daughter, she doesn't have a choice but to. Dream is putting up this front like she doesn't give a fuck, but deep inside, she does. She went and purchased a fucking house for Ginger's ass. A nigga is pissed because she did the shit without talking to me first. On the other hand, understand her feeling the need to do that on the strength of trying to build a relationship. I know how Ginger moves, so it's imperative I have a talk with her. She needs to know off the rip I won't play with her ass when it comes to Dream.

Dream buying a fucking house for her will do nothing but make her think Dream is sweet. We all know my baby ain't for none of the bullshit. At the same time, she's been looking for her mother forever. I believe that want for a mother will make her blind to the obvious. I may be wrong, but I'm not taking any chances. It's enough bullshit in the air right now. We don't need any more motherfuckers with ulterior motives against this family.

The moment I pulled up to Ginger's house, I became angry. She had a porch full of fucking crackheads. I needed to calm myself down before I got out of the car. A nigga wanted to murk Ginger's ass. She was supposed to be getting ready to head to the rehab. Dexter had found a place, and she agreed to go. Watching her basically hit the pipe out in the open angered the fuck out of me. I hopped out of the car with the quickness.

"Aye! Get the fuck off this porch right now!" I had my gun out, so they all scattered like roaches. Swiftly I walked up on Ginger and knocked the fucking pipe out of her hand.

"What the fuck is you doing?" Before answering, I pushed her ass inside of the house.

"Sit the fuck down, Ginger, and don't say shit."

"Wait a goddamn minute! This is my house, and I don't have to listen to you and nobody else. Your ass is paying me for my crack you knocked out of my hand. Damn it, Fendi! Why would you do that shit?" This bitch literally had tears streaming down her face. All I could do is look at her and shake my fucking head.

"I don't give a fuck about this being your house. I also don't give a fuck if you overdose on that shit. What I do give a fuck about is Dream? You see, what the fuck you're not going to do is play games with her."

"This is why I didn't want to agree to shit with Dexter. Now you think you gone tell me how to behave with the daughter that I gave up for adoption. All of y'all got issues. It's a reason why I gave her up. She deserved better than to be raised with a mother like me. Look at her now. She's about to be married into a rich and ruthless ass family. I would say she's doing just fine."

"You have no idea what Dream went through behind that shit. Raped and molested at every fucking foster or group home she ever went to. Don't sit your ugly unfit ass right here and talk on how good her life is. She went through hell to get where she is today. You don't have the fucking right to speak on her at all. Dream had a rough ass life growing up. Now she's living the life she deserves, and for some reason, she felt the need to buy your ass a house."

"Let me cut you off right there. I gave that deed back to Dexter to give her. I'm a fucked-up bitch, but I would never take anything from her. I don't deserve it. Please understand me. I don't want anything from Dream. Dexter gave me an ultimatum, and I'm headed to rehab in a little while. I really don't want no problems at all. You wasted your time coming over checking me about Dream. I can assure you I have no intentions at all of being her life."

"Why the fuck wouldn't you want her in your life?" I spoke through gritted teeth. That last statement she made angered the fuck out of me.

"It's pretty hard looking at a child that looks like your rapist. It's even harder when that rapist is your father. So, you see, I didn't want to give my daughter away. I had to. I couldn't bear looking at her everyday knowing where she came from." Ginger pulled out a cigarette and flamed it up.

I believed her. It was something about the way the words came out. Ginger can't be trusted for shit, but she was telling the truth.

"Why you just didn't tell her that when she came over here?"

"I've never repeated that shit to anyone. My mother was deceased and I was left in the care of my father. We had no other family, so the paternity of my daughter was never addressed. I only told you because you're coming over here like you want to kill me. I'm trying to stay as far away from Dream as I can. You don't have to worry about me bringing any bullshit to your doorstep. Plus, I'm not trying to deal with your crazy ass grandma. You know she came over here earlier and threatened to slice me from A to Z if I hurt Dream. Two visits from two crazy ass Alexander's in one day is enough for me."

I couldn't help but laugh hearing my granny had slid through. That's my baby right there. She does no fucking around behind us at all.

"I think that you're going about this shit all wrong. Instead of trying to create distance from her, you need to sit her down and talk to her. After that, you go your way. Dream needs that missing link. She needs to know that it wasn't her fault. Get clean, Ginger. I promise you will love being a mother and grandmother. That might just be what you need to live a good life. Look around you. You're in a house that's falling around you. That house is still yours. I'll buy you whatever car you want when you get clean and stay clean. I came over to check your ass, and here I am offering you a car. This is for my baby. She deserves to know the truth."

"I don't want no gifts from y'all. I'm going to rehab because I'm tired. You can drop me off right now. I'm ready. When I'm clean, I'll sit down with Dream. I don't want her to ever see me like that again."

"That's what I'm talking about. Get your shit, let's go."

"I'm going like this. I can't take anything inside anyway. Dexter will bring whatever when my counselor reaches out to him."

Ginger followed me out of the house, and we headed over to the rehab center. From where I was sitting, she looked ready. However, Dex has been doing this shit with Ginger for years, so hopefully, she's serious this time.

"HEY, BABY!" I missed you so much. Dream ran and jumped on me the moment I stepped inside the house.

"I missed your sexy ass too."

We passionately kissed as I walked and carried her into the living room. A nigga couldn't help but squeeze her ass cheeks. The shit felt like too big ass pillows. A nigga don't ever mind eating her ass with all that fluffiness. I sat down on the couch with her still straddled on me.

"How was your day?"

"It was cool. How about yours? Where are my kids at?"

"My day was long as fuck. I had meetings with building inspectors all day. Your grandma decided to keep the kids. She told me I needed a break. You should have seen me racing out of her house today. It's just you and me tonight, baby! We can fuck whenever, wherever, and as loud as we want to."

Dream started placing kisses all over my neck as she tugged at my pants. She really did miss a nigga. Before I knew it, Dream was on her knees, giving me the best top ever. I couldn't do shit but lay my head back and let her do her thing. She was sucking, slurping, and motorboating the fuck out of my dick. I palmed the back of her head and made her speed up the pace until I came full force.

"You missed a nigga for real!" I managed to say as I tried to gather myself. My ass felt like a nigga who had just got his virginity took. Dream had never sucked my dick like this before. The shit had me shook as fuck. At the same time, the shit felt so good. If this were our first time meeting, I would have happily given up my bread and watch.

"Hell yeah! Now let's go upstairs so I can ride my dick."

"What the hell done got into you? Since when you turn into a super freak?"

"Stop fucking playing with me, Fendi. You know I've been a freak, but I can't drop all my moves on your ass at once. I have to space that shit out. Now let's go upstairs, and I'll show you how to fuck me Chinese style."

"Hell, nah! I like doggy style. You can keep that foreign shit. Let me find out you trying to seduce me." I smacked her on the ass as we headed up the stairs to our bedroom.

"Nigga, please. I seduced you the moment you laid eyes on me, and you know it. Now come drop them draws. My pussy has been craving to feel you."

As soon as I got ready to come out of my clothes, my emergency phone rang. I quickly answered, seeing that it was my grandma. The life drained out of me hearing her say that our daughter had stopped breathing.

"What's wrong, baby?"

"Put your shoes on we have to get over to the hospital. Granny had to rush Chanel to the hospital."

"What? Is she okay?" Dream asked as she panicked.

"Calm down and let's just get to the hospital."

During the entire ride, we both prayed that she was okay. I swear a nigga couldn't win for losing. Like I know, I'm not living right, but kids were off-limits behind my bullshit. I've never prayed so hard in my life. I just pray God heard me and kept my daughter here with us.

"CALM DOWN, bro. She will be okay." Givenchy was trying everything to calm me down, but I couldn't. We had made it to the hospital, and they still hadn't come and said anything.

"That's Baby Chanel. She's a hard body, bro. She has Alexander blood running through her veins," Prada added as he patted me on the shoulder.

The entire family and our workers were at the hospital. The emergency and family room were all filled up. That shit felt good because we needed this support.

"They need to tell me something about my daughter before I snap." Dream jumped up, but Miyani quickly grabbed her.

"Come here, baby." I quickly pulled her into my embrace and let her cry on my shoulder. As fucked up as I am, I needed to be stronger for her.

"What are we going to do if she doesn't make it? Your grandma said that she was blue when she found her. It's all my fault. She was wheezing last night, so I gave her a treatment. This morning she seemed fine, so I went to work."

Dream was crying, and I was tearing up. Ever since our daughter had been diagnosed with asthma, we had been on edge. At only two years old, it was pretty bad for a kid her age. Both Dream and I had been closely monitoring it, so I understand why she feels the need to blame herself.

"It's not your fault." I looked in the distance and saw our daughter's doctor headed toward us.

"Please tell me something good, Doc?"

"Mr. and Mrs. Alexander, Chanel is going to be okay. She had an asthma attack in her sleep. That's why she was blue when her grandmother found her. We had to intubate her when she was brought in, and her oxygen levels are improving. We want to keep her sedated so the oxygen can work its magic. Your grandmother got her here just in time."

"Can we go see her now?"

"Yes, Ms. Alexander. Please come with me."

"Go ahead, babe. Let me go let my granny know she good." I kissed Dream, and she rushed off with the doctor.

"Told you, bro. My niece tough as fuck!" Prada proudly said as he and G dapped it up.

"I'm going to go with Dream. Love you, bro." Miyani and I exchanged hugs before I rushed out to the emergency where my grandma was. She didn't want to sit back in the family room.

"Is my baby okay? When I laid her down, she was fine."

"Don't cry, granny. She will be okay. She had an asthma attack in her sleep. That's why she stopped breathing. Right now, they have her sedated just to help with the oxygen flow. Calm down, gangsta. I've never seen you cry, ma."

My brothers and I had her surrounded. Hell, we were about to cry because that's something that she doesn't do.

"That hurt hit different when it's one of y'all or my grandbabies hurt. All I got in this world is my grandkids. God has got to take me first because I couldn't live without any of you."

"Awww! Big Bad Gladys is crying," Prada said as he started kissing her all over her face. G picked her and gave her a bear hug.

"Put me down right now! Y'all play too much. I'm serious." She smiled.

"That's what I like to see. Come on so you can go back and see her." I grabbed my granny hand, and we headed back to see my daughter. It had been years since I held my grandma's hand. I was young as hell when my mother left, so I can't remember much.

This moment right here makes me angry with Chanel. She's our fucking mother, and she should be here. Then again, my granny is our mother. Speaking of my mother, Chanel's ass still hasn't reached out to us regarding this situation with Versace and her whack ass baby daddy. That nigga hasn't been back around, but we were still keeping eyes on Versace around the clock. If what that nigga said was true, he'll definitely be back. If he knows what's good for him, he'll take his ass back to Haiti and take that shit up with Chanel. Team Supreme don't honor outside agreements!

IT HAD BEEN a couple of days since my daughter had to be hospitalized. I was thanking God that she was going to be just fine. On the other hand, a nigga was worried. She would most likely have to deal with asthma for the rest of her life. Nevertheless, we're grateful God kept her here. Lord knows I would have lost my mind if she hadn't.

Now that my daughter is out of the woods, its time I have a talk with Dream. I've been dreading the fuck out of this shit. The trip to Atlanta was much more than a business trip. We headed down there to make sure that our compound was ready for our move-in. My brothers and me had made the decision to move our families down there until shit blows over. The government is out for blood, and this time around there will be no getting out of we don't find a way inside. The fucking pigs got this case sewed the fuck up, so we can't take any chances.

"I'm ready, baby. How do I look?" I bit my bottom lip as Dream did a full-body spin in front of me.

"You look good as fuck."

My baby was looking good as fuck draped in her nigga! She had on a sexy Fendi print dress with the heels to match. It warmed a nigga's heart to see how iced out my baby was. She was giving Gucci's bitch Keyshia Ka'oir a run for her money on the ice side. When all this shit is over, I'm making it my business to cop her a buss down that's gone make hoes want to cry. I went from wanting to kill her ass for stealing my watch to buying her one. This definitely mirrors some of that bullshit they be reading.

"Thank you. Now, tell me where we going?"

"I can't tell you. It's a surprise. You ready to go?"

"Yes, I am. Miyani said the kids are sleeping, and she gave Chanel her medicine. I'll call in thirty minutes and check again."

"No. You won't. Miyani's holding the kids down ain't no need for you to worry. I want you to enjoy this surprise I have for you. Tonight, I need you to focus on me."

I pulled her close and wrapped my arms around her waist. After engaging in a passionate kiss, we headed out the door. As excited as I was, a nigga couldn't help but be nervous. Dream was going to lose her shit when I told her everything.

We were riding down Lake Shore Drive listening to the music in silence. Never in my life had I been so speechless with talking to a woman. Then again, Dream wasn't just any woman. She was the mother of my seeds, my future wife, and my best fucking friend. The last thing I want her to do is hurt or worry behind me.

"This is my surprise?"

"No. Your surprise is up the street. I need you to put this blindfold on."

"Oh my god, Fendi! The suspense is driving me crazy. You better not be bullshitting with me either."

"I swear I'm not bullshitting you, babe. A nigga just wants to give you something nice. Let's just say it's a push gift for giving birth to my seeds. You deserve it all, baby. She turned around in the passenger seat, and I placed the blindfold on her eyes. A minute later, we were pulling up to the surprise I had for. I got out of the car and walked around to the passenger side to let her out.

"I don't even know what it is, and I'm crying already. You've done nothing like this."

"Welcome to Club Dream!" I whispered in her ear as I gently removed the blindfold.

"No fucking way! Oh my god! You bought me a club."

"You've always expressed to me how much you love making your own money. I've watched you bring Club Bliss to the forefront of the club scene. Our numbers are through the roof because of you. I found the layout in one of your journals you left open, and I immediately took it to a crew, and they've been working on it around the clock."

"It's exactly the way I envisioned it. I can't believe you did this for me. Nigga, I love you so much. Now tell me what the fuck is going on!" Dream kissed me on the lips then roughly pushed me away.

"What the fuck are you talking about. Ain't shit going on. A nigga just wanted to do something nice for your ass." I was trying my best to keep on a straight face, but her ass was making it hard. Dream swore she could tell I was lying just by looking into my eyes.

"That's the thing. This shit is more than your regular nice. You don't do shit like this with your mean ass. Since your ass came back from Atlanta, you've been nice as fuck."

"You sound crazy as hell right now. So, what you're saying is you want me to be a fucked-up nigga. This some bullshit!" I quickly spoke and walked out of the club with Dream following close behind me. She had fucked up the whole surprise with her detective shit. She can't just go with the flow.

"Don't walk away from me, Fendi Alexander!"

"Don't be out here yelling at me like you done lost your fucking mind! Get in the car, Dream, and we can discuss this shit." Of course, she rolled her eyes and stomped off like the brat she was. Right now, is not the time for her to be going off on me.

"Before you pull off, let me say what the fuck I need to say. Don't disregard me."

"Go ahead, Dream." I threw my hands up out of frustration and let her talk.

"First of all, I'm not an ungrateful bitch, so please don't mistake my anger. I love the fact that you bought me a club. You've always given me nice things. A bitch appreciates the fuck out of that shit, but by the same token, I know when something is off. All this shit is off, and it's been off for a minute. Do you honestly think I sleep next to you every night and know nothing about you? You've been overly nice to me with your mean ass. You don't have a romantic bone in your body. That was a dead giveaway.

For the last couple of months, everybody has been moving really funny. What the fuck is going on, Fendi? Don't lie to me. I swear I'll bite the fuck outta your ass again."

I took a deep breath before putting the shit out there on the table.

"Before I say anything. I just want you to know that this club is something that I've been working hard on for months. This surprise was definitely from the heart and not a guilty gift. For the last couple of months, shit has been real crazy. You just gave birth, so the last thing I wanted was to put more on you. We found out that the government is building a whole new case against Team Supreme. It's in the works they just haven't handed down any indictments.

To be on the safe side, we decided to move you, Gavin, Miyani, and the kids down to Atlanta until shit blows over.

"Really, Fendi? You didn't think this was something that should have been discussed with me? I love Chicago. What the fuck was you thinking giving me this damn club knowing you would be sending me to Atlanta. By the way, I'm not going any motherfucking where."

"Yes, the fuck you are going, and that's definitely the end of discussion. There is no negotiating this shit. I want my family tucked away and safe from Chicago. Now listen to me Dream and listen well. If anything happens to me, your name is on everything. All my important papers are in the wall safe, insurance policies too. No matter what happens, you keep running the businesses and handle shit."

"Why are you saying all of this? You're scaring me, Fendi." Dream was now shedding tears. Her ass needed to stop because, in a minute, she would have me tearing up. Tears weren't needed right now.

"Stop all of that crying. You my gangsta bitch! Promise a nigga right now that no matter what happens, you will hold shit down. I got you rocking my chain for a reason. You're not a weak bitch, so stop crying. Now promise me you gone hold shit down for a nigga!"

"I promise."

"That's my girl." I grabbed her chin and kissed her like I was headed off to prison at that moment. Honestly, I could be headed to prison any day, so I was getting all the kisses and pussy that I could.

NINE

PRADA

"What am I going to do, grandma?"

"You're going to take your ass home and tell Gavin everything. This baby was before her time, so there is no need for her to be mad. If you keep this shit a secret, then she has every right to go oops upside your motherfucking head! Don't keep putting this shit off. You've had those results for over a week now. That's a week too fucking long for my liking. Gavin is a good woman, and she loves you. Telling her would be in your best interest. You know that she's been through a lot. Don't add that type of stress to her life."

I knocked back the shot she had poured for me and stared at the paternity papers in disbelief. This bitch Oni really had a baby by me. If it wasn't one thing, it was another. A nigga can't catch a fucking break. After finally getting my shit together, here comes some bullshit. Gavin had been so damn excited about planning the wedding. Now, I don't think there will be a wedding at this point. It's like a nigga can't catch a fucking break around this motherfucker.

"I promise I'm going to tell her tonight. First, I need to go see this bitch, Oni. I haven't heard from that bitch since she called bragging about the results.

"I have to make it my business to make a trip to see that bitch. She's playing games with the wrong one. If she thinks that child is her meal ticket, she's sadly mistaken. I'll kill her ass and take that baby from her. You make sure you let that hoe know what the fuck it really is."

Granny was so pissed off this damn baby was mine. Hell, I was too. I've always wanted kids just not with a cum catcher like Oni. I wanted all my seeds to be with Gavin, but God had other plans.

"I'm ten steps ahead of you. I love you, and I'll call you later."

I kissed her on the cheek and headed over to see Oni. If that bitch jumps stupid, I'll fuck around and put a bullet in her head today. That bitch gets no passes for playing with me. I paid her ass to get a fucking abortion, and she acts like she got it. A nigga didn't think shit about it when she disappeared. If anything, I was relieved I didn't see her ass anymore. For three whole years, she'd known she had a baby by me and didn't come forward. The crazy part is she came back and started working at the club like it was nothing. All I could do is run my hand over my face in frustration. It felt like I was being pulled in all directions. My only concern is making sure I get shit straight with Gavin. It fucked me up that I had to tell her all this fucked up shit. Besides telling her about my daughter, I have to come clean about moving her out to Atlanta. A nigga was about to have it bad like Usher.

"I SEE you got the results. Are you ready to be a father now?" Oni opened her front door and stepped to the side for me to enter. The look on her face was one of satisfaction. She played my ass, and I had to deal with it. At the same time, she needed to tread lightly.

"Watch your fucking mouth, bitch! Don't talk to me like I'm some deadbeat ass nigga. I didn't know shit about you being pregnant. Watch how the fuck you handle me with this situation before I put a bullet in your fucking head."

"Mommy! I'm ready to go to the pool."

My heart skipped a beat when a little girl appeared that looked like a little grown woman. Her hair was all braided up with beads on the ends. The two-piece swimsuit she had on was far too revealing for a three-year-old. Her nails and toes were painted, and the fact that she had on sunglasses and a purse was too much. Oni over here grooming her to be grown at a young age. She looked cute but unacceptable for a three-year-old baby. Knowing this was my seed, that shit was going to change immediately.

"Okay, baby. First, I want you to meet somebody. This is Prada, and he's your daddy."

Oni removed the glasses from her face, and then I could see that she was mine. She had hazel eyes like my grandma. The shit was so crazy. My granny would be crazy about this one. Hell, I hadn't even spoken a word to her, and I was crazy about her.

"Come here and tell me your name." I kneeled and waited for her to come to me. At first, she was reluctant, but then she slowly walked to me.

"Don't be scared, baby. Tell him your name."

"Tiyonni Alexander."

"That's a pretty name for a pretty girl. It's nice to finally meet you." The moment I placed a kiss on her jaw, someone started banging on the door. I quickly looked at Oni and pulled my gun out, thinking this bitch was setting me up.

"Why are you pointing that gun at me, Prada? Did you not forget she's right here?"

"Shut the fuck up and answer the door!"

I walked closely behind her as she opened the door. Before she could fully get it opened, it was kicked in. I damn near had a heart attack when Gavin started beating the fuck out of Oni. Miyani came in and cornered Oni so that Gavin could really get her.

"Bitch! You got me fucked up!" Gavin was punching Oni like she was a professional boxer. All you saw was her head popping back and forth from the punches.

"Beat that bitch ass, Gavin!"

"Mommy!" Hearing my daughter cry made me quickly try to break the shit up.

"Aye, what the fuck! Stop this shit, y'all. Don't do this bullshit in front of my daughter!" I didn't mean to yell or push Gavin. It was harder than I wanted, and she ended up falling back. By the way she clenched her chest, I knew it hurt her.

"Don't push my fucking sister! Why would you do her like that?"

"Come on now, sis. You know I didn't mean to push her that hard. I love Gavin. Just let me explain. Please baby! Let me explain!"

I rushed over to where she was, and she pushed me back.

"Get your hands off of me!"

"I'm about to call the fucking police right now! Get the fuck out of my house right now. I can't believe you let them fight me in front of our daughter, Prada. Please leave my house.

"You not gone call nobody. Take her in the back so I can talk to my wife."

"Nah, you good. We don't have shit to talk about. This ain't over, bitch! It's on site every time I see you hoe! Bring your ass on, right the fuck now, Prada!" Gavin yelled loud as fuck, making a nigga jump. Shit, I had never seen her this fucking mad. Honestly, I was scared to go the fuck home with her crazy ass.

"You still standing here?" Miyani asked with her hand on her hips. She and Gavin were on some bullshit today.

"I'm telling my brother on your ass." I pointed in Miyani's face as I walked out of the door behind Gavin slow as fuck. She was standing by her car now with her gun out. I swear if she shoots me, I'm shooting her crazy ass back.

"I don't care. Both of y'all got my sister and me fucked up! Now take your ass home before we jump your ass next." Miyani rushed past me and exchanged hugs with Gavin before leaving in her car.

Miyani and Gavin were lucky I wasn't the old high ass

Prada. Both of their ass would be laid the fuck out behind testing my gangsta. It's a damn shame I love Gavin so much. No other woman has ever been able to carry on around me this way, and I continued to fuck with them.

Gavin waited until I got closer to her car before she jumped in. She peeled off on my ass and damn near hit me in the process. Yeah, she was losing her fucking mind right now. Without hesitation, I hopped in my car and followed her ass to the crib. As I followed her, Oni started blowing up my damn phone, but I couldn't answer her right now. My main priority is trying to fix this shit with Gavin. It felt fucked up being pulled in two directions at once. A nigga definitely had to make this shit up to Tiyonni. Just thinking about how she was screaming and hollering had me feeling fucked up. I didn't even get a chance to do what I went there for in the first place.

When I pulled up to the house, I hit my blunt a couple of times before going inside. Gavin was in rare form, and there was no telling what she was on with a nigga. I left my phone in the car simply because Oni was blowing it up. Gavin would probably fuck around and shoot my ass.

Walking inside the house, I observed Gavin pacing back and forth with her gun still in her hand.

"You need to calm your ass the fuck down! I understand that your ass is upset, and you have every right to be, however, don't play them gun games with me. I guarantee when I get on that gunplay with you, your ass won't like it. Now put that shit down and talk to a nigga."

I walked over to the bar and poured me a shot of D'ussé and knocked it back. Gavin stared at me a minute before walking away from me. I pinched the bridge of my nose, trying to calm down. Her ass was about to make this shit hard on a nigga. Before going in search of her, I knocked back another shot.

My heart started to hurt, watching her pack her clothes. Gavin was really trying to leave and a nigga. She had me fucked if she thought I was about to let her walk out on me.

"You're wasting your fucking time packing that shit! On my granny, you not going no motherfucking where." I snatched the suitcase out of her hand and launched it across the room.

"Bye, Prada! Take your ass back over there to that bitch house. You walking around here knowing damn well some bitch was saying that she had a baby by you. The moment you found out you were supposed to come home to tell me. I should never have been served paternity papers at my office."

"Wait a minute! What the fuck you mean you were served with paternity papers?"

"Yes, nigga, that bitch had someone deliver it to me. Imagine my surprise when I open it and pull out a paternity test. You have a three-year-old daughter, Prada. What the fuck am I supposed to do knowing that?"

"The same motherfucking thing I did with CJ. I accepted him from the gate as my son. Don't stand here acting like being in my daughter's life is the worst thing ever. I had no idea she even existed. When I found out a nigga was in shock. I didn't feel like telling you until I knew for sure. I paid that bitch money for an abortion. Hell, she disappeared after that. The next time I saw the bitch she was working at Club Bliss. Versace hired her not knowing who she was. She brings in a lot of high-end clientele so there was no Fendi was going to let her go.

"I don't give a fuck about who she is and how all of it came about. Nor does it have anything to with you having a daughter. You have been extremely good to my son, so it's only right I treat your daughter the same way. I'm not reacting like this for shit. The fact of the matter is your ass is a liar, Prada Alexander. You got those results back a week ago. Nigga, you have walked your ass around this house all week, and not once did you say anything to me."

"Aye! Get your finger out my fucking face before I bite that bitch! You act like I fucked that hoe or something. You came in the door swinging, and not once did you give me a chance to explain."

"I came in there swinging because that hoe played with me. She should never have sent that shit to me. That bitch served me some papers like I know her ass. Nigga, you never should have kept this shit from me."

"Hell yeah, I kept that shit from you. It didn't feel good coming home telling my future wife I had a fucking daughter."

"Well, it didn't feel good being served the news in front of our staff. The next time you call yourself saving face for me, don't! Keep shit all the way one hundred with me so that I can decide whether I can handle it. You see, this shit is about you lying and keeping shit from me. The fact that the little girl is yours is a blessing. At the same time, it doesn't change the fact that you and her mammy played with me". She grabbed the suitcase and started back trying to pack. I quickly snatched it out of her hand.

"Look, you pissing me off steady packing and shit. You not leaving me, Gavin. It's death do us part. Don't forget that shit."

"Are you stupid, nigga? We're not married." That was it. I couldn't help but slam her ass on the bed.

"I don't give a fuck if we aren't married. You're my motherfucking wife, Gavin! A piece of paper doesn't mean shit. I'm not feeling the way this headed, so I'm going to stop it before we both do or say some shit we will regret. I wasn't lying being sneaky. I didn't tell you in an effort to protect your heart. Do you honestly think I would keep some shit like that from you to hurt you? I love your ass too much for that. It's just so much going on right now, and I'm being pulled in all directions.

"Get off me, Prada! I need a break from you." She had tears falling down the sides of her eyes. I understood her being pissed about Oni having her served. At the same time, I didn't know I had a daughter.

"What the fuck you mean you need a break? I don't think you're listening to me. You can be mad at a nigga all you want, as long as we're mad under the same roof. I'll give you your space and sleep in one of the spare bedrooms. I'm sorry for not telling you, and I hope you can understand why I went about it that way."

I tried to kiss her on the lips, but she quickly turned her head. She was going to make this shit hard for a nigga. Her ass needed to come to grips really quick. I have a daughter, and there is nothing I can do to change that.

This shit had the potential to get worse before it gets better. I still hadn't told her about the great possibility of moving down to Atlanta. I hated to leave her, but I knew she needed to cool off. Heading back to the car for my phone, I had missed calls from my brothers. I had planned on heading back over to Oni's, but business came first. Oni was definitely going to see me first thing in the morning. The bitch is headed toward the morgue being on bullshit.

TEN

GAVIN

This shit with Prada had me all in my feelings. I honestly wasn't mad at him about having a daughter. How could I be? He knew nothing about her. This shit is bigger than that. It's the principle that has me all fucked up in the head. He should have come home and told me the moment that bitch popped back up on the scene. I was so fucking happy he had left the house. I've never been so mad in my life. I threw myself across my huge California king bed in deep thought about this shit. The more I thought, the more hurt I became. If he lies to me about this, he'll lie about anything. I've been through so much, and my heart can take no more.

Carlo took me through too much, and I can finally look in the mirror and love the woman staring back at me. You don't know how much you've lost yourself until you become unrecognizable to yourself. That man ripped away my very existence. Prada helped me find myself. Although loving him through his personal issues was a lot on me, I took that shit head-on and stood up in the paint. There were days I needed him, and he was unavailable. At the same time, he was there for me when I needed him the most. Why he thought he couldn't come tell me this shit is beyond me.

The fact that the bitch sent that shit to Alexander Enterprises pissed me off. Imagine me showing the office spaces to potential clients, and I'm being served fucking paternity papers. That shit was embarrassing as fuck. That's the main reason why I'm pissed. He could have prevented that bitch from doing that simply by being honest. Prada Alexander has got to understand that this shit unacceptable. If I forgive him off the rip, I'm opening doors for him to do the shit again. Without any more hesitation, I packed me some clothes and left. He thought I was playing when I said I needed space.

"BITCH, you need to stop playing and take your ass home!" Miyani said as she laid across the bed. It had been three days since I left the house. Prada had been blowing my phone up. His crazy ass had the entire family calling me, and I was ignoring them too.

"I might go home tomorrow or the day after. Hell, I don't know. I love it here."

"Yeah, this shit is nice. Why the fuck you didn't tell me you had this condo?" I took a deep breath and got ready to reveal a secret I had been keeping to myself.

"To be honest, I own this entire building. Apparently, Carlo has several properties across Chicago that he had in my name. I knew nothing about this shit. When I learned about it, I immediately let them people know we were divorced. When he signed those papers, I immediately filed them. Now they're telling me they have no record of the divorce, which is some bullshit. As you know, they can't find him. That motherfucker had my name on all types of shit, offshore bank accounts, and everything. Thank God he was a damn dummy and never changed his pin codes. I've transferred over fifty million dollars into my accounts. I'm an even richer bitch today than I was yesterday. By the way, make sure you buy yourself something nice with the money I put in your account."

"Trust me, bitch! That ten million will be spent accordingly. Now, does Prada know about this shit?"

"No, and I don't know how to tell him. He's going to be mad about it."

"I am so confused right now. Here you are held up in this condo and not at home, all because he didn't tell you about a bitch possibly having a baby by him. Yet, you're keeping important shit from him that he should know."

"Don't remind me, bitch!" I flamed up a blunt and hit it a couple of times. He needed to know about this shit, but at the same time, I wasn't ready for his action.

"Seriously, a lot is going on with Team Supreme. This

morning G shut down all the blocks. He was so damn angry that I didn't even ask questions. Please tell him," Miyani pleaded. For the first time in a long time, she looked so worried.

"Shit's got to be serious if he's doing that. Is shit still good with y'all?"

"Since our last fight, we've been in such a good place. The sex is better than it has ever been. I can honestly say that we're good relationship-wise. Despite all that, Givenchy is not himself. I can feel it at night while he sleeps. My baby hasn't been right since I was locked up. He's here with me physically, but mentally he's a thousand miles away. I just wish he would let me in and let me know what's going on."

Before I could respond, my phone started ringing. I handed Miyani the blunt and grabbed it. I immediately pressed ignore on Prada's ass. A bitch still wasn't ready to talk. I quickly placed my focus on my sister. Clearly, she was stressed out behind this shit going on. As we all were. I was even more confused because Prada was keeping me in the dark about things as well. Outside of the paternity issue. He hadn't been honest with me in regard to what's going on with the team.

"Team Supreme is a beast at what they do. Trust me. They got this shit. Don't worry about, bro. He's a beast at what he does. Team Supreme is his life. Every decision he's making is for the greater good for us all. Stop worrying. Let's head over to Ms. Gladys' house. She made banana pudding, and I need to get CJ."

"I'll ride with you and come back to get my car later."

I quickly changed the subject. Clearly my sister was worried. Honestly, I was too. They were keeping us in the dark about something. Givenchy shutting down blocks did nothing but let me know she was about to get real or it already did. We've been through so much I've become numb to the shit. As crazy as it sounds, I've placed my mother and her bullshit on the back burner as well. She's still on the run, and she better stay gone. The bitch has caused all this fucking drama and now she's in hiding. Everybody's looking for her ass since G put a million-dollar bounty on her head. That old hoe is hiding real good and Butch's retarded ass is right with her. That bitch never loved my father, and I can't wait until they murk her ass.

"DON'T GET SCARED NOW, HOE!" Miyani said as she laughed. We pulled up to Ms. Gladys' house, and Prada's car was parked out front.

"Bitch, I'm not scared, and Prada's not stupid. If he hits me, are you going help me fight his ass?" I was dead ass serious, and she was laughing.

"I don't know, sis. That nigga's been on a rampage since your ass has been gone. It's only been three days, and he's been acting like you've been gone for years. Prada is gone fuck your ass up. You already know I got you, sis."

Without a doubt, I knew she was going to ride with me. A bitch just needed to make sure. We finished a blunt then got out of the car.

"They must be having a party or something. You hear the music?"

"Hell yeah! You know they ass be having random ass gatherings. Let's go around back. The closer I got up to the backyard, the more scared I became. It was a good thing a bitch had on her VaporMax. I'm going to take off on his ass if he jumps stupid.

The moment we walked into the backyard, I wished I would have waited to come. It was as if they were having a big ass barbecue. The entire team was in the yard. They had spades and dominoes going. Of course, there was a dice game going on. Scanning the crowd, I had to do a double take. My heart plunged, looking at Prada's daughter sitting on his lap. I tried my best to keep calm, but there was something about the way he was smiling down at her. Reality had really set in that quick. Someone had given him something that I hadn't. Just seeing them together shifted my mood and had me overthinking.

"You okay?"

"Yeah, I'm good. I'm about to get my baby and go back to my condo." I lied to my sister. My ass was not okay. In that moment, it felt like I was going to crack in a million pieces.

"I thought we were coming for banana pudding?"

"Girl, fuck that banana pudding!" I walked off on her and headed inside the house. It was time for me to get my son and head the fuck out. If I didn't leave soon, some shit was sure to kick off.

When I walked into the kitchen, my son was sitting in a highchair next to G-Baby with his fat self. Ms. Gladys was feeding them spaghetti. Without hesitation, I tried to grab him, but she stopped me.

"Don't bring your ass in here with that bullshit. That baby was before your time. I didn't raise my boys to be deadbeats. Now, the paternity test proved he is the father, and he's stepping up like the fuck he should. Don't be mad at him, Gavin. He had no idea about her."

It was time for me to go. Ms. Gladys was taking up for Prada, and it irritated me.

"I'm not the type of woman who gets mad at children. I

am the type of woman that gets mad when the man she plans on spending the rest of her life with lies about having a daughter.

"Hold up now! You can drop that attitude shit with me. I know the type of woman you are. If you were anything less, you never would have stepped foot in my fucking house. Now you and I are different because we bonded before you ever laid up with Prada. I know when you are hurt so, you can't fool me. At the same time, running away from him won't change the fact he has a daughter."

Leave it to Ms. Gladys to make a bitch shed tears.

"I know it won't. Thanks for keeping him for me, and I'm sorry if I disrespected you in any way."

I quickly wiped the tears from my face and grabbed my baby. Without another word being spoken, I headed back out to my car. Miyani was all over G, so I knew she was leaving with me. I saw Prada's daughter running around playing, but I didn't see him. That was my cue to get the fuck out of dodge before he had a chance to fuck with me.

"Fuckkkk!" I said underneath my breath. Prada was leaning up against my car with a steel bat.

"What you thought I didn't see you come in?"

"I wasn't trying to hide. Move so I can leave. You need to go back in there with your daughter." I sounded childish, but I didn't care. Prada swiftly took the bat and bussed the passenger side window out.

"Your ass is not going anywhere. I advise you to take my son and go back into the house. I've been looking for you and calling your ass for three days straight. Bitch, you got me fucked up thinking you going to leave a nigga behind some bullshit. Take your ass back in there, or I swear I'll destroy this bitch."

"I don't give a fuck, Prada. Tear it up. Your ass is paying

for it too!" I was acting tough on the outside, but on the inside, I was crying. He had just got me the brand new black on black Maybach. I loved the car because he had it designed just for me.

"You right. I brought this bitch so I can tear it up." He just started going crazy and tearing my damn car up. My son was so scared that he was shaking and crying. That made me start to cry too. His ass always found a way to go too damn far when he's mad.

"Stop this shit right now, Prada!" Ms. Gladys tried to walk up on him and get the bat, but she had to jump back. He was swinging the bat erratically and damn near hit her. That's when everyone started rushing him.

"Man, bro, you're going too far. Your ass almost made my granny fall," Givenchy said as he walked up on Prada and snatched the bat. He and Fendi started tussling, and they all ended up brawling.

"Y'all need to stop this shit!" Ms. Gladys was trying her best to break them up. She was no match for all them big ass niggas, trying to hold Prada down. He was like the Hulk, and he was morphing by the second.

"Here, babe, take my car and get Gavin out of here." Givenchy practically pushed me out the damn way.

They were all finally able to subdue Prada. G, Fendi, Butta, and Gunna all had to hold his crazy ass down. I knew that I should have been headed to the car, but there was a part of me concerned about him. I just wanted space to deal with things. This was not what I meant to come from me needing that.

"Don't let her leave, sis! I swear to God you better not leave, Gavin! On my life, if you leave, we done. I didn't do shit, and you handling me like I did something wrong. That's my daughter! Deep down inside, you want me to choose! Talk to her, Miyani. You know she wrong as fuck for this shit. Get the fuck off me! I'm good. If her ass wants to leave, she can." He yanked away from them and walked away from everybody.

All I could do was try to calm my baby down. He was clinging to me for dear life and crying.

"Come on, Gavin. Let's go. This is too much on CJ." Miyani took my son from my arms and cradled him. She walked off toward G's car, and I slowly followed behind her.

My heart and soul were hurting from Prada's behavior. I climbed in the backseat with my son because there was no car seat in Givenchy's car. Before driving off, I watched Prada come back out to the front of the house, trying to calm his daughter down. Tears streamed down my face. It hurt me seeing that. My son was crying, watching Prada act a fool, and not one time did he cradle him or try to soothe him.

"Don't cry, sis. You know he just hurt because you dipped on his ass. Are you going back to the condo or home?"

"I don't know. Just get me the fuck out of here. I can't believe that man just destroyed a two hundred-thousand-dollar car."

"Well, believe it. Make sure you never call my man crazy again. That nigga Prada is a couple of bricks short of a building. You lucky that nigga beat that car's ass instead of yours. You can't keep running from this situation. In my heart of hearts, I know you love that man, and you're scared. That little girl will not change the way he feels about you or CJ. He loves him as if he were his own. I'm always on your side, but I do think that you need to go home. Laying up in a condo you inherited from your ex-husband that he murked won't help shit. Plus, your ass knows that you aren't about to leave that man. Just be the bigger person and go home."

"Why do I have to be the bigger person? He's wrong, Miyani. Prada kept that shit away from me. That's why I'm mad. It's real fucked up that he thinks I'm mad that he has a daughter."

"I'm not saying he's right. What I'm saying is. Sometimes we women can wave the white flag. The shit is strictly in an effort to keep the peace. I'm your sister, so I'm going to keep it one hundred. I watched you when we entered the backyard. The moment you saw him with his daughter, your whole mood changed. If the little girl isn't the issue, you need to speak on what it is. I can honestly see why he thinks that. For Christ's sake, Gavin, you've been gone on the man for three days with no communication. He is feeling fucked up, sis. Stop crying. I'm going to take you to the home you share with that man. Fix this shit, Gavin!"

Miyani had raised her voice at me, and just that quick, I stopped crying. I had to really get a good look at her because she had got emotional.

"Why do I have to fix it?"

"Cause they're the only family we have outside of you and me. Neither Prada nor G is perfect, but they love us. They've given us love when our own parents didn't. We're a family now. Team Supreme, right?" Tears streamed down her face as she drove. I really didn't want to go home, but in an effort to keep the peace, I decided to.

"I'm going to go home, but you need to tell me why you're so emotional?"

"I'm emotional because I feel like Givenchy is slipping away. I feel like everything is changing right before our very eyes. I just feel like we need to hold on tight to the one thing outside of our babies that keep us going. I'm not telling you to fold or let him have his way. I'm simply saying hold on to your family. You and I both know how easy it is to lose your family within the blink of an eye. I didn't mean to get emotional. I'm just trying my best to be positive in a situation that I'm not sure of."

For the rest of the ride, we were silent. The music wasn't even on, and that was a first. I didn't know what was on the horizon. I just prayed we could get through it. We've been through more than enough. It was about time we get some peace and our happily ever after.

As Miyani drove, I sat in deep thought. The only thing in my mind was getting to my happy place with Prada. I'm tired of shit being good for a minute, and then it's all bad. In my heart, I know that Prada is who I want to spend the rest of my life with. I just don't want to put up with certain shit in the name of having a family. Miyani must have forgotten family ain't shit either. At the same time, I don't want to live without Prada, so I'll take the high road this time. I'll do it because I love the fuck out of Plus, I'll do anything if it helps Team Supreme. All relationship bullshit to the side, we're the motherfucking truth! United we stand and divided we fall.

GIVENCHY

I sat back in my office chair, smoking a fat ass blunt in deep thought. It killed me to shut down all illegal Team Supreme operations, but in an effort to keep my loyal foot soldiers out of prison, I had to. The move out to Atlanta wasn't permanent. It was a temporary action just to get my family from here while we fix this shit. In the upcoming weeks my brothers and I will be headed out to Panama for business.

A nigga hated to put a hold on everything, but it was a must. The good thing about this shit is that we have enough money to last us a lifetime. That's why it's always good to have legit money pouring in along with your illegal money. I don't know what Team Supreme would do without Miyani, Dream, and Gavin. They've been running shit on the legal side, and the trips to the bank have become more frequent. That's why I'm pissed we have to send them out to Atlanta. As much as I need them here handling shit for my brothers and our cause, their safety is more important.

I'm not sure how Gavin and Dream feel about the shit, but I can tell Miyani hates it. Nevertheless, she's not complaining. She has been being overly supportive and helping me deal with this shit. It makes a nigga feel good and bad at the same time. I'm happy that she wants to hold me down to the fullest. On the other hand, I feel fucked up because she's putting herself to the side.

Although we made up from the argument we had, I can't help but feel fucked up. When I met her, she was at peace, yet I came into her life and disturbed her spirit. It's a must I give her the peace that she deserves. This life with a nigga is way too fucked up for Miyani. She's a classy ass lady on all levels. The hood wife life is beneath a woman like her. She belongs with an executive nigga. Instead, she wants to be with a Team Supreme nigga. It's only right I go above and beyond to make it the best life she has ever had.

Besides dealing with this fucked up case, I still hadn't found Melissa. It was as if the bitch had disappeared off the face of the earth. That was another reason I wanted to get Miyani out of Chicago. I didn't feel comfortable with her and the kids being out here with that bitch on the loose. I have some of my best men on the case, so I'm sure we'll find her ass soon. Miyani's acting like nothing has transpired between her and Melissa. It's weird because she wants me to stop looking for her. She knows I won't stop until that bitch is cut up into tiny ass little pieces. The shit has me in deep thought.

On a brighter note, I finally spoke with Chanel. She insists that Versace's bitch ass husband was lying on her. At this point, I don't know who to believe. Actually, I don't give a fuck either way. He had better stay his bitch ass away from my fuckin' sister and nephew. She's literally living her best life and making her own bread. She doesn't need any distractions right now. The best thing she ever did was stay here and let Chanel take her ass back to Haiti. I love my momma, but it's bound to be bullshit whenever she is involved.

"Aye, bro! Murray's out here. He says he got something for us."

Hearing Fendi say that made me quickly follow him out the door. I hope it was something good and not no more bad news cause the last thing I needed right now is more bad news.

"What you got for me, Murray?" I asked as we dapped it up.

"It better be good too. Your ass is always bringing us bad news," Prada added.

"The news I have today is a little of both depending on how you feel. From my very reliable source, I now know who the informant is and has been for a long time." Murray slid folders across the table to my brothers and me.

"I knew we should have killed that bitch when she said fuck Team Supreme," Prada stated.

"We should have known it was her and that hoe Niara.

They moved too fucking deceitful. I'm really ready to off them hoes." Fendi paced back and forth as he spoke.

I sat quietly staring at Nettie's picture. Niara being labeled a rat meant nothing to me. It didn't hurt. Nettie, on the other hand, that shit cut deep with a nigga. My family took that dyke bitch in, and she turned on us in the name of pussy. I guess I'm more shocked that I missed the signs. Nettie never gave off any bad vibes.

"Do you know how long she has been an informant."

"Now that I don't know, but Nettie has been the driving force between this new indictment. We never had this conversation. Please move clean. I'll be in touch."

"Here, Murray. This is ten grand for you. For the first time, you gave us some shit we can work with." We laughed as Prada dapped it up and handed him an envelope filled with money.

"Yeah! Good looking, Murray. We have a trip out to Panama next week. I'll reach out to you when I make it back. We appreciate you for this."

Without waiting to see him out, I headed back to my office. Shortly after, Prada and Fendi came in and sat across from me. I took a blunt from my candy dish and flamed it up.

"So, how are we moving with this shit, bro?" Prada asked.

"We know how you feel about Nettie, and we ready to off both of them hoes, but if you want this one, we'll fall back." I passed Fendi the blunt after he spoke his piece.

"I'll handle it. Make sure you put Gunna and Butta on both them bitches. I want to know what the fuck they do every fucking second of the day. This trip to Panama is coming up, so we need to be focused on that."

"No doubt Bro. Are we still in agreement to keep granny out of this?"

"Hell yeah, Prada! Don't tell her shit. I don't feel good making her worry at all. Dex will be looking after her and Versace while we're away. Once we handle shit in Panama, then we will let her know," Fendi stated.

"Sounds like a plan. Let me get out of here. I promised Gianna I would watch *Belly* with her. She'll have a fit if I miss her family movie night." My daughter was a trip. She didn't like kiddie movies at all, and it was driving Miyani crazy.

"I hope you know your ass is over there raising a future Harley Quinn." Prada laughed, and I didn't see shit funny.

"I'll shoot both of you niggas talking about my baby. She's gone be a gangsta like her daddy and run this shit. Watch what I tell you. I love you niggas, and I'll see y'all Sunday at dinner. Make sure Gunna and Butta hit me up the moment they put eyes on them hoes."

"We got you," they said in unison, and I headed home.

For the first time in a long time, I was headed home with the load a tad bit lighter. That small piece of information would help us out in a big way.

I PINCHED the bridge of my nose, trying to calm down. The e-mail I had just received had me confused and livid at the same time. Apparently, my presence was being requested at a black and white affair for the Bosses Round-table. Attached was also my official letter of acceptance into the faction. This had Miyani nosey ass written all over it. I tried my best to calm down. I couldn't, though. I distinctly told her now wasn't a good time. Why the fuck would she do some shit like this? Right now, is not the time for me to be doing this shit. I had to attend because not attending would clearly be seen as disrespect. Real gangstas don't move fraud like that. Thug Inc. is rare around this motherfucker. Getting an invitation to anything with their stamp on it is a big deal. Seeing that I'm something like a big deal, it was only right I pull my chair up to the table.

I needed to knock back a shot or two to calm down before talking to Miyani. She has no fucking idea how angry I am at her for doing this shit. I'm sure she did the shit with good intentions for a nigga. At the same time, she overstepped her boundaries when she did that shit. This is the one time I can't really be easy on her. She has to know that certain situations are caused for her to be my wife and know her place. The shit could be a matter of life or death. Team Supreme has a lot at stake right now and fucked up decisions can cost us everything. The Bosses Roundtable is a great asset to have on my resume. I know nothing but greatness will come from being a part of it. Having said that, it's just bad timing for a nigga.

After facing a blunt, I walked through our home in search of Miyani. I heard loud music playing which led me inside of her dance studio. Before walking in, I fell back and observed her practice with Gianna. The classical music was relaxing and calming. Just seeing how much Miyani and Gianni loved each other made me relax. I intended to spazz out on her, but I decided not to. The sight before me was everything.

Miyani and I locked eyes, and she smiled. That same beautiful ass smile that I fell in love with.

"Good job, Gianna. Go take a bath and get ready for bed. Tomorrow we will work on your hip-hop piece."

"Okay, mommy." A look of shock went over both me

and Miyani. That was the first time I actually heard her refer to Miyani as her mother. I could tell Miyani was taken aback as well.

"How was practice?"

"It was hard, daddy," Gianna spoke like a true drama queen as she hugged me.

"Okay. Daddy will take you to the spa tomorrow for a day of relaxation."

"Good, Cause lord knows I need it." She walked off like the grown woman she was.

"She is a trip." Miyani laughed. I quickly grabbed Miyani in my arms and hugged her tight.

"No, G. I'm so dirty and sweaty." She was trying her best to wiggle out of my hold, but I squeezed until she relaxed.

"You know I love you, right?"

"Yes, Givenchy. I know that you love me. Do you know that I love you more than anything in this world?"

"Absolutely, that's why you go behind my back and send that RSVP back to that nigga Thug." Her eyes widened because she wasn't expecting me to say that.

"Please don't be mad at me, G. Baby, from the moment I found out what it is that you really do, you talked about this. You wanted your faction to be a part of that shit. Let me tell you something. I've done my research on them. Trust me. This is great for us. Stop thinking it's not the right time. This may just be the perfect time to join the Bosses Roundtable. You are the infamous Givenchy Alexander. This is God's plan for you, for us, and Team Supreme." Miyani was talking that good shit to a nigga. She thought she was slick laying it on thick to keep me from spazzing. The shit worked too. She had my dick harder than a motherfucker!

"I'm glad you're so passionate about this shit. Go out

and find you the baddest fucking evening gown and shoes you can find. We've been invited to a black-tie event next month. I think mingling with the other wives will be good for you. Come make love to me." I placed a kiss on her forehead and led her back to our bedroom.

With all that was going on, I would rather fuck my baby brains out as opposed to arguing and going to bed mad. This time I'll put faith in my woman. For the first time, I'm seeing her strength with this hood wife shit. This event is exactly what she needs to be attending. My baby is ready to make her mark up there with the rest of the finest hood wives in the game.

TWELVE
MIYANI

I laid in bed, staring at the ceiling in deep thought. My mind was going into overdrive thinking of my life and where it was headed. The feeling of Givenchy wrapping his massive arm around me relaxed my nerves. A slight smile formed on my face as I snuggled closer to him. While he lightly snored, I contemplated on this next move that I needed to make alone. In order to get the peace of mind that I desire, I must confront the shit head-on. It's time to finally get rid of the bitch known as Melissa. From the moment I walked out of jail, I vowed to get that hoe. This shit was personal to me. It was bigger than anything she had done to Team Supreme. It was about her being my fucking mother and treating me like a bitch on the street.

I've been going over the shit in my head repeatedly, and I'm still drawing blanks. I know most people are saying, Miyani give it up. That bitch doesn't love you, and she never will. Trust me. I know that. Despite all that, she's supposed to love and protect me. That's why finding her and Butch has been my main goal. Both of them owe me an explanation. I didn't ask to be here. You don't give birth to a child then mistreat them. That bitch was going to provide me with an explanation before I snatch her life. Not telling Gavin was fucking with me, but she didn't need to know what I was doing because she would stop me. Plus, dealing with Prada and his craziness was enough on her.

Honestly, there was no one I could tell about this. They all would stop me. If Givenchy knew what I had been doing, he would probably lay hands on me. This would definitely send him over the edge. That's because he looks at me as a soft, well spoke, beautiful ballerina. He has to understand that things have changed drastically. My outlook on life is different these days. I've been through too much shit to be the same Miyani he first met. I have murder on my mind and vengeance in my heart. In order for me to get to my happy place, I have to handle my own shit.

I could have been told Givenchy where Melissa and Butch were hiding out at. Instead, I hired my own security team. They had been keeping an eye on them until I was ready to make my move. It had been hard, but I was able to keep on my game face. Givenchy was smart as fuck, and if anything were off about me, he would know. He had been so engrossed in Team Supreme that it gave me the space I needed to do some digging. It appears the city of Chicago is indeed corrupt as a motherfucker. Who knew this city was knee deep into human trafficking? I knew that the shit existed, but not to the extent that I know of now.

The best thing my father, Malcolm Mills, did was leave so many files in his home office. I don't know how Melissa missed it because it was right inside the desk. After his death, we found out that we inherited our childhood home, which was the house they still resided in at the time of his death. Clearly, Melissa was in a rush when she left the house. It was so much evidence. I had been spending hours going through the many journals that he had kept. The black book his attorney gave me was nothing compared to the shit I had in my possession. So, you see if a bitch blinks at my man wrong in this city, I'm ruining their fucking existence. The government thinks they can just dismantle some shit they didn't build. My man wants to be great and change this fucked up city, but they won't let him. When it's all said and done, Team Supreme will reign down fury around this motherfucker.

Yeah, it's official, a bitch had to hang them dancing shoes up and put on her boxing gloves.

In the files left behind, I found several deeds to properties with Gavin and my name on it. That's where I started at. One, in particular, was a beautiful Victorian home out in Glencoe. It fucked me up in the head when I realized it was the home she always wanted to move out to. We would only go there in the summer to get away. She hated that my father loved living in the city. It was no surprise to me when I learned that's where she and Butch were practically living.

After doing my own research, I found out them nasty motherfuckers were running an illicit sex ring in one of the wealthiest suburbs of Chicago. I cringe thinking that I have their sick ass blood running through my veins.

The reason sleep was hard to find was because I was ready to make my move. It was time for me to confront them head-on. All day I had been contemplating following through with it. After speaking with G, I knew the shit needed to be handled immediately. My man needed my undivided attention for this event. The last thing I needed was feeling like Melissa was somewhere in the shadows to fuck shit up. Having eyes on them is not enough to keep them from further retaliation against us. It's better to get rid of them now. This shit has been going on for too long.

"GOOD MORNING. It's Saturday, beautiful. Where are you going?" Givenchy asked as he sat up in bed.

"Good morning. I'm sorry that I woke you up. I'm actually headed to look at some properties Malcolm left. I'm going to be meeting up with the appraiser. It shouldn't take too long, though.

"Why you just not telling me about this? Don't you think this was something we should have discussed? I don't see why you need to go look at that shit. Let the appraisers and the real estate team handle all of that. That's what the fuck you pay them for. I ensure that you have help so that you won't have to get out of bed on a Saturday."

Damn, why did he have to wake his grumpy ass up?

"I know that. It's just I want to go look at this specific one myself out in Glencoe. You know I've been asking for a house either there or in Winnetka. I promise I'll be back in a couple of hours. The kids are with Versace. Take this time to get you some rest." I love you. I quickly placed a kiss on his lips and rushed out of the room.

That nigga was so mad. Today was not the day for Givenchy to be preaching to a bitch. My mind was made up. I couldn't afford for him to knock me off my square. He was out until five this morning, so I know he's going back to sleep for a couple of hours, which was all the time I needed to handle the task at hand.

About an hour later, I pulled up on my security team. Bakari and Benny Boom were some of my old friends from grammar school. It was only by coincidence that they were some foot soldiers for Team Supreme. I hired them to keep a watchful eye on Melissa and Butch.

"You sure about this?" Bakari asked.

"I've never been more sure about anything in my life. Thanks, for looking out for me. I know it was hard doing this without Givenchy's permission. After today you won't have to do anything else. Here is fifty thousand for each of you. I will not take no for an answer."

"Now, you know we can't take no money from you. This one was on the house. Go in there and handle your shit. We'll be out here watching your back." I knew Benny would refuse the money.

"Your ass is taking this money. I'll be right back out." I threw a duffle bag filled with money at their feet. The niggas had no choice but to take it now.

"If you're not back out here in ten minutes, we're coming in."

"Before heading up to the front door, I grabbed a family photo album. Growing up, Melissa was always big on appearances, and we took photos often. I brought the bitch a reminder to show her how fraud she is. The lady in these books is not who she portrayed herself to be.

As I proceeded up the long driveway, I couldn't believe there was no security. One would think they would have this place locked down like Fort Knox. This just further proves that the bitch thinks she is invincible. There's a fucking bounty on her head, and she's in the suburbs acting like she can't be touched. Her ass is in for a rude fucking awakening.

I exhaled as I walked up the steps to the front door. Without wasting another minute, I knocked on the door. I knew that someone was inside because of the cars parked in the driveway. That and the fact that lights were on throughout the house. This bitch had a lot of nerve laying up in this house as if she owned it. My phone started going off in my pocket, and I quickly shut off the ringer. the door swung open at the same time.

"Can I help you?" a woman asked in a maid's uniform. It was no surprise she had a maid taking care of her. The world would end if her ass had to lift a finger.

"I'm looking for Melissa Mills?"

"Ms. Mills isn't taking any visitors today. Can you leave your name and I'll let her know you dropped by?" Before I could say anything, Melissa came into view.

"Let her in, Consuela. You can leave now. I'll see you tomorrow."

"Yes, ma'am." The maid stepped to the side and let me in. She damn near ran, trying to make herself scarce. We both stood in the foyer, staring at each other before she broke the silence.

"I'm sure Team Supreme will be coming in at any minute. Let's get this shit over with," she spoke casually, and it irritated me.

"I'm here by myself. I thought I would give you a gift from Gavin and me."

"I don't want it. I see your scar healed well." She sipped from her champagne glass like it was nothing. I just wanted to attack her and beat the fuck out of her. Instead, I kept my cool and got down to why I was there.

"Baby, who was at the door?" Butch appeared, and I can tell he was shocked to see me.

"It's our daughter. She and Gavin brought their mother a gift."

"It's not just any gift. It's a photo album from the house you shared with my father, Malcolm Mills. You know the man that you poisoned to death."

"Don't be disrespectful, Miyani. Your father is standing right here." I damn near fell out laughing at this bitch. She was serious as hell referring to this man Butch as my father.

"This nigga right here is not my father, just like you are no mother of mine. I'm content with not having either of you in my life. In any case, I deserve to know what I did to you. Why would you give birth to me and then turn around and mistreat me?"

"I don't care about none of this shit. You see, Melissa, this is what the fuck I'm talking about. Bitch, you always got some shit brewing and making me a part of it. All this shit is your fucking fault. I distinctly told you this is why I didn't want to come out here in the first place. Tell this girl the truth so that I can get on with my life!"

"Sit the fuck down and answer my wife's question!"

My heart damn near leaped out of my chest, looking at Givenchy. *How in the fuck did he know I was here?* A bitch kept her composure and didn't show any fear. Now wasn't the time for him to preach to me. I needed to prepare myself for his wrath because he was definitely going to go off on me later about this shit.

"I don't want no problems with you, Givenchy!" Butch's old coward ass looked like he was about to shit on himself. I couldn't believe this was who she wanted to be with all these years. Malcolm was a pussy, but he had more heart than this motherfucker.

"I knew he wasn't too far behind. So, much for coming alone."

"Shut the fuck up! You wicked low life, bitch! Who the fuck are you to speak on how I move? Bitch, you are not qualified to question me about anything with your unfit ass. Last time I checked, you watched while some bitches whooped my ass. That was coward as fuck, especially since you're the one with all fucking hate up in your heart. What type of woman hates her own daughter? Are you that fucking jealous of me that you would purposely hurt me?"

"Everything is always about you. I knew it would be my biggest regret the moment I found out I was pregnant. Butch, remember when I came to tell you I was pregnant? What did you say to me?"

"Right now, is not the time for you be playing these fucking mind games, Melissa. Back in the day, everything you did was to make Chanel jealous. You got pregnant by a man that didn't want you. It was business with us. You were supposed to get the bitches and bring them to me to pimp out. Instead, you wanted to run shit. That's why we're here now. All you had to do was stick to the fuckin' script. When will you get it through your fucking head that you will never be Chanel Alexander? You're competing in a league where you will never compare. I told you to get a fucking abortion. It's not my fault your silly ass didn't do that. I went away for about fifteen years and come home to you on the same shit.

From the moment I got out, you've been on bullshit. Aren't you tired of this shit? You've lost everything behind trying to be somebody that you're not. All in an effort to prove a point to a woman who is still prospering besides all the shit you've done to her.

In case you didn't get the memo, Chanel is running shit over in Haiti. Meanwhile, you've burned so many business relationships. Now your ass is stuck out in the suburbs pimping out suburban housewives to the last of the politicians who still fuck with us. I know I'm about to die today. Before I leave this world, I just want you to know that my heart has always been with Chanel."

"Damn, nigga, you got heart to confess some shit like that! It's good to get shit off your chest before you leave this world."

"Nigga, do you actually believe that I think so highly of you? Butch, you are a weak ass pathetic excuse of a man. I used your ass all these years. It's funny how you stand here bitching up and running off at the mouth. Big bad Butch stand up to every fucking body but them fucking Alexanders. You're standing here speaking so highly of a woman who never wanted you. Your heart was with her, and her heart with Slim. Don't stand here flattering yourself trying to make it seem like you're some boss ass nigga. She never wanted your ass. You were just a pawn in her game against Slim, and you know it.

That's the difference between you and me. I stand up in the paint behind everything I do, unlike you standing here acting like you better than me. You've been down with every plan from the start. So, tell your daughter just how much of a hand you had in this bullshit too. I can't believe you standing here talking about how you never loved me. I'm the bitch that put money in your pocket, nigga."

"I don't give a fuck what you put in my pocket. Bitch, you owe me. Whatever hand I had in anything is because you were hell bent on me helping you. Honestly, I don't believe her or that other girl belongs to me. Your ass was loose as a goose back in the day. Anybody can be that girl Daddy. I just went with the flow in an effort to get money. You not fooling no one but yourself. Tell the truth Melissa! You treat her like shit because you don't know who her father is. I'm sorry you want it to be me, but I seriously doubt it!" Just hearing them two going back and forth let me know I would never get any clarity. It was just time to wash my hands of the whole situation and move on.

"Fuck this shit! I didn't come here to kill either of you. At this point, I'm sure you will kill each other. I came here to get closure from both of you and to put you out of my fucking house. Yes, this is my house, and bitch, you know it. All this shit y'all taking about still doesn't answer my fucking question. At this point, I don't even care. I am well within my rights to murder both you unfit ass people, but neither one of you are worth the bullet."

"Talk to me, beautiful! This is your show. I'm just here for moral support." It relaxed me to hear Givenchy say that.

"You have until the end of the business day to get off my fucking property! If either of you ever come near my family again, I'll make sure to let my man put a bullet in your head. Leave the state. In case you missed the memo, you've been exiled. Don't try me, Melissa, especially, with the knowledge I know about you trafficking everything from coke to underage boys and girls for sex. Leave and never come your disgusting ass back. Come on, baby." I grabbed G's hand, and we walked out of the house.

"Baby, we can't leave them alive! I know you're trying to be the bigger person but not right now. I'm sorry, I got to off them motherfuckers for everything they put you through." G tried to snatch away from me, but I found the strength to pull him away from the house forcibly.

"Cover your ears."

"Huh? Man, you tripping. I have to go back and kill they ass." I held in my laugh because he was looking at me so crazy as I pulled him away.

"Just cover your ears."

I walked closer to where Bakari and Benny was, and that's when I took notice of Prada, Fendi, Butta, and Gunna. I should have known them nuts weren't too far away from Givenchy. They all make me sick. Who the hell told them to mess up my plan? Once we were a good enough distance away from the house, I discreetly pressed the button on the key fob in my hand.

"What the fuck?" Givenchy yelled, trying to gather himself from the house exploding behind us.

"I told you to cover your ears." I couldn't help but laugh at all them niggas trying to gather themselves after feeling the effects of the explosion.

"Damn, sis! You cold with it, huh? That's what the fuck I'm talking about!" Prada yelled, jumping up and down.

"I thought you didn't want to kill them?" Givenchy asked.

"Did you really think I was going to let them mother-fuckers live? You don't know me at all, Mr. Alexander?"

"You damn right, I don't know you. How in the fuck do you know about making bombs?"

"It's always the pretty ones that be crazy! I knew she wasn't no damn ballerina."

I laughed as Fendi shook his head at me. They were all really looking at me in amazement, and it was hilarious.

"Let's just say I learned while bonding with my mother-in-law. Let's get the hell out of here."

Without hesitation, I quickly hopped into my car to leave. Givenchy was fuming but didn't want to show it right then and there. In the rearview, I could see all of them trailing behind me. He had just given my ass a pass for that Roundtable situation. There is no way he will let this shit slide.

"BITCH, I still can't believe you went and did that shit without us. You know I've wanted to kill your momma since the first day I met her."

"Man, listen, I just wish I could have been there to see the explosion. Just knowing that Melissa's dead and in hell where she belongs make me sleep easier at night. Bitch, you still wrong for not telling me, though. She was my sorry ass excuse for a momma too."

Both Dream and Gavin were getting on my nerves about this shit. They were supposed to be here having a celebratory drink with me, but instead, they were cussing me out.

"I told you bitches it was something I had to do on my own. It's bad enough Givenchy found out about it. Cut a bitch some slack, please.

"Speaking of G. I know he went in on your ass."

"That's the thing. He hasn't said a word to me about it. Not one word. He's acting like it never happened. The nigga got me scared as fuck. A full day has passed by, and G has yet to say anything regarding what I did. It's driving me crazy waiting for him to go off. I've never wanted to be cursed out so bad a day in my life. He needed to get this shit over with and stop torturing me. This is all a part of his madness."

"That's how Fendi's crazy ass be. He's trying to calm down before he addresses it."

"It was nice knowing you, sis. G is going to kill your ass." Gavin's ass was really laughing like something was funny.

"You bitches ain't no help at all. I only invited your ass over here for moral support."

"You should have let us in on your secret. We would have all been in trouble with you—you're on your own, sis. I'll see you tomorrow at Sunday dinner. That is if Givenchy doesn't kill your ass first," Gavin said, causing her and Dream to fall out in a fit of laughter.

"Both of you bitches get out of my house." I started pushing them hoes toward the front door. They had to get the fuck out thinking everything was a joke. Them silly bitches were still laughing getting put out.

"No, really. I'm happy you stood up to her ass. I love you for finding the strength not to let them win. Don't worry about, G. That man is more proud of you than anything. You better be a boss ass wife, Mrs. Alexander." Dream placed a kiss on my cheek and walked out of the door.

Now, I just need Givenchy to address this shit so I can move on with my life. Getting rid of Melissa and Butch had freed a lot of my time up. Now I could spend more time with the kids and handling the family businesses.

LATER THAT NIGHT, I found myself lying in bed once again, overthinking. Now, I was wondering if I had done the right thing. The last thing I wanted was for him to not be able to trust me. He needed to know that I was trustworthy. The decision that I made didn't go against him and his wishes. It just helped me get rid of the baggage that was holding me back from the peace I needed. It was one less situation weighing him down. If anything, he should feel a sense of relief.

I sat up after hearing the security alarm beep. Listening to the code being entered in, I relaxed a little. It was Givenchy coming in for the night. My son stirred a little in his sleep, so I tried to be as still as possible. Both him and Gianna was in bed with me as usual. The idea of being a mother of two still hadn't really registered with me. Sometimes I had no clue how I had managed to get the job done, but I did. They both made it so easy to be their mom. Having a supportive man like Givenchy made the shit a breeze. We really wanted for nothing. In all honesty, we really did have a beautiful life. Hopefully, I didn't fuck it up going behind G back.

"Let them have the bed. Come fuck with me in my man cave," Givenchy spoke as leaned up against the doorframe in our bedroom.

I slowly got out of bed successfully without waking up the kids. Lord knows if they woke up now, they would never go back to sleep. My mind wondered as I followed him down the stairs. The stance he had let me know he was ready to address the Melissa situation.

"Look before you go off."

"Shhh! I'm not about to go off on you. Listen to me, Miyani. You did what the fuck you had to do. Who am I to tell you how to go about murking your mother? Plus, I've been known what you were up to."

"Say what now?"

"You see, you're the one who really doesn't know me, Mrs. Alexander. I didn't make it this far in the game for shit. First of all, you can never hire people that work for me. They will never handle business for you without permission from me. I'm well respected but feared by most. You're precious cargo, beautiful. Every man in this city knows to be at your beck and call if you request it. Free of charge."

"I can't believe this. All of this time, I've thought I've really been ten steps ahead of you." Givenchy grabbed me and leaned my body into his. We were face-to-face with one another.

"Don't ever think you're ten steps ahead of me in a game I created. I'm proud of you, Miyani. You've shown me that you can handle your own and protect our kids. It makes me relax a little knowing that if anything happens to me, you could survive."

I immediately cut him off because I was tired of him talking like this. It was as if he thought he was going to die or something.

"Why are you saying this? I told you I didn't like hearing you talk like that."

"Nothing is going to happen to me. Stop panicking when a nigga says that." He kissed me on the forehead and flamed up a blunt.

"You promise you're not mad at me."

"No, beautiful, I'm not mad at you. However, in light of this situation, I think it's important we make that move to Atlanta.

"Why so soon? There is so much paperwork I have to do for the businesses. How can we just move down there on a whim?"

"It's not on a whim. We've planned it out carefully and

methodically. Trust me. This move is what you need. You need a break from the big city."

"I can't believe this."

"Well, believe it. A lot is going on, and I need you and my kids away from Chicago for a while. Don't fight me on this because then I'll be pissed off at you. I've been calm and let you do shit your way. Now, it's time to fall back in line and follow my lead. Do we have understanding, Miyani? I really need you to understand where I'm coming from with all of this."

Reluctantly, I gave in even though I wasn't feeling the shit.

"Okay, G, I understand. Just promise me nothing will happen to you. You're scaring me with the way you've been talking. I don't know what I would do if the kids and I lost you." My ass didn't mean to tear up, but the very thought had me emotional.

"Shhhh! You guys will never lose me. I'll be with you forever and even after that." G wrapped his arms around me. All I could do was hold on tight. He was shielding me from something, and I didn't like it one bit. His heartbeat was so calm as we stood in the middle of the floor, holding each other. He's been letting me off too easy, and nothing about Givenchy is easy. That's how I know something is not right. I closed my eyes and prayed that God kept us covered.

"Why the hell you still in the bed, Dream? I thought you were going to see Ginger today?"

I rolled my eyes and put my head underneath the covers. Fendi had been on me for the longest to at least have a sit-down with her. I only promised to do it to shut him the fuck up. That shit only made him get on my ass more.

"I'm not going." I placed the pillow over my head and prayed he would go away and leave me the hell alone.

"Get the fuck up!" He yanked the covers off me, and it made me quickly sit up.

"I'm serious, Fendi. I really don't need to talk with her. As long as I have a relationship with Dex, I'm good."

"No, the fuck you not good! From the moment I met you, all you did was talk about knowing where you come from, and now you know who your mother is but refuse to sit down with her. What's really good?"

"Why are you so serious about this all of a sudden? Not too long ago, you forbid me from even looking for her. I'm confused, babe." This man was going on a rampage about me getting my feelings hurt behind this, yet now he is all for me having a sit-down with her.

"I just want what's best for you."

"What's best for me is loving the family that took me in. I don't need to build a relationship with someone I never had in my life to begin with."

"Maybe you need to throw caution to the wind and find out why she didn't keep you. You'll be amazed to find out the truth without making perceptions. I love you, Dream. Please go to the rehab center and visit Ginger. She's thirty days clean today." Fendi kissed me on the forehead and walked out of the bedroom.

This shit had me so frustrated, not to mention nervous about it. That was more of the reason why I didn't want to have a sit-down with Ginger. What if she said something I didn't like, and I kicked her ass? Fendi knows I need anger management. The last thing he needs to do is force me into a situation that makes me angry. It was now or never with the situation. I just prayed she didn't tell me some weak ass excuse as to why she gave me up. Rehab or not, I'm going to kick her ass.

"I DISTINCTLY TOLD these folks no visitors," Ginger loudly spoke as she walked into the meeting hall.

When she locked ass with me, she stopped talking. Her demeanor let me know that she wished she could turn around and walk out. Honestly, a part of me hoped that she did. It bothered me that I really didn't want to do this. She looked one hundred percent better than when I last saw her.

"What brings you here, Dream?"

"What the hell you think brings me here? Look, what I'm not about to do is sit here and play games with your ass. I told Fendi I didn't want to this shit, but he insisted that I come."

"I told him I didn't want to as well. That's one pain the ass of a man you got on your hands. When you walk out of here, tell him I don't need him coming up here every day getting reports of me. I'm going to kill him and Dexter's motherfucking ass. I'm in here trying to get clean, and they fucking with me. I'll deal with them later. I'm sure you have some questions for me. Let's get this shit over with. My next meeting is in thirty minutes. Ask me whatever you want to ask me, and I'll answer it."

"I guess the main question is the obvious one. Why? Why did you give me up for adoption?"

A huge lump formed in my throat. I quickly swallowed in an effort not to choke. My body became so flushed as my heart raced. It was beating so fast. The feeling of fear had taken over me. Ginger reached across the table and placed one of her hands on top of mine. It caused a shiver to go through my body. For the first time, I felt a touch from the woman that gave me life. It was a confusing feeling.

"I'm sorry for not being a mother to you. I wish I could have had the strength to be able to be your mom and not look at you with hate. It's pretty hard looking at this beautiful baby girl that looks just like your father." I quickly removed my hand from hers, hearing her say that.

"What?" Ginger quickly wiped the tears that had fallen.

"As hard as it is for me to admit it. It's true. My father raped me from the age of seven to seventeen. You were a product of that rape. Many times I had become pregnant by him, but he found out in time. After four forced abortions in some damn basement, I became pregnant with you. Before I knew it, I was five months pregnant and too far along in the pregnancy to get one. Baby, I was homeless when I gave birth to you. There was no way I could bring a baby back with me and live on the streets. Why would I do that to you? I knew that you would have a much better life with someone else other than me.

By that point, I was on that heroin train, and a bitch was not ready to get off it. I know that sounds fucked up. That shit was the only thing that helped me cope. My mother passed away and left me in the care of my father. No one knew that he had me living as his wife and his daughter. For years I believed that what he was doing to me was normal. There was no other family to step in and intercede on my behalf. When I walked out that hospital and left you, I cried for days. That was the hardest day of my life. I'm sorry for everything that you endured at the hands of me leaving you. It's good to know that Ms. Charlotte made sure you kept the name I gave you.

"Wait a minute? You knew my momma?"

Ginger's eyes lit up like she was offended. I had to give her a look that reminded her that she might have birthed me, but she wasn't a mother to me. Ms. Charlotte was my saving grace. She is and will always be my mother.

"Absolutely. She was a nursing assistant when I gave birth to you. It was her support that helped me to make the decision. I knew she couldn't take you then, but she promised when she got things together, she would come for you. I'm just happy she kept her promise."

I was absolutely floored listening to this. For a minute, I wanted to question why Ms. Charlotte never told me any of this. It would have definitely helped me to lighten the mental load that weighed on me for so many years.

"I never expected to hear all of this today. It's so over-whelming. Be that as it may, I'm glad we had this conversation. All I have ever wanted was to know why and where I came from. It's heartbreaking to know that I'm a product of rape, and the man who gave me life is also my grandfather. It hurts me knowing that. I can only imagine the hurt you've had to deal with. I couldn't be mad at you anymore if I wanted to." I reached back across the table and placed my hand on top of hers.

"Wrap it up, Ginger!" her counselor yelled across the room at us.

"Thanks for coming to see me. Hopefully, one day I'll get to meet my grandbabies. Fendi gave me these pictures of them last week."

"He visits you?"

"Since the day he dropped me off. Both him and Dexter have been making sure I'm doing the right thing. I'm thirty days clean, and I'm ready for the next thirty. Fuck these drugs! I want my family. I love you, Dream. I promise never to let you or Dex down again." We both stood, hugging each other until the counselor cleared her throat.

"Get yourself together in here, and when you walk out those doors, you'll be set."

"I got you, Dream." Ginger quickly walked off, and I stood watching her until she disappeared behind the doors.

The nervousness I felt had now subsided. A sense of calm had taken over, and I relaxed. It felt good to talk to Ginger. It felt even better hearing her want to change. I just hope and prayed that she was serious about being clean. If she was, I had so many plans for her. I was going to give her the life her nasty, disgusting ass father took away from her. It's really some sick ass niggas out here. It's bad enough these people like touching on little kids, but for a father to do that shit to their own seed is beyond me. Any man that violates a child deserves to be tortured and chopped into pieces.

On the drive home, I couldn't help but think about Fendi. He was so damn sneaky. No wonder he has been so hell-bent on me forming a relationship with Ginger. All along, he had been involved in everything that was going. Conversations between him and I played out in my head. He knew that I was a product of rape. I'm not mad at him about not telling me. After all, it wasn't his truth to tell. I guess I can say the same about Ms. Charlotte. She just never came clean to me because it wasn't her place. That and the fact that she wanted to protect her Dream.

Sadness came all over me. It was imperative I clean off her grave and bring some fresh flowers. I had to let her know I found Ginger and a man that loves the deepest parts of me. She would flip knowing I had children, especially, since I vowed never to let a nigga knock me up or lock me down. Look at me now. Fendi's trying to knock me up for the third time and definitely got this pussy on lock.

While heading home, I received a call from Ms. Gladys telling me to come over. I did not have time for her shit today. Every time she calls out of the blue inviting me over, it's some bullshit. The last time she called me, I went with her to collect a gambling debt, and Ms. Gladys ended up beating the shit out of some lady old lady with her own cane. I'm not going with her ass, no matter how much she pays me. Ms. Gladys is going to get us all knocked with the bullshit she be on.

ABOUT AN HOUR LATER, I was pulling up to Ms. Gladys' house. I was surprised to see everybody's cars parked out front. It must be an impromptu meeting for the family. Walking inside the house, I went in search of everyone. They were all in the conference room. Fendi, Givenchy, Prada, and Ms. Gladys were standing. Miyani and Gavin were sitting next to each other with papers in front of them.

"Come in and have a seat, baby," Fendi greeted me and led me over to a seat next to Miyani. He then placed papers in front of me.

"What the hell is going on?" I asked while looking down at the paperwork. Reading over it, I looked up, locking eyes with Fendi. Looking over at Miyani and Dream, I could tell they were just as confused.

"I called you girls over because it's imperative we take precautions. In light of everything the family is facing, we want to make sure you all are secure.

"So, what does this mean? I take your last name, but we aren't legally married?" I asked.

"I'm in the middle of planning our wedding. What marriage is no longer on the table?" Miyani asked as she pushed the papers away from her. My girl was sad as fuck. As she should be. These niggas were trying it today.

"Come on now, beautiful. You know damn well we are having our wedding. It's just that right now is not a good time for any of us to get married. Y'all have been holding shit down for us. What we're doing right now is giving you all security. You'll be giving up your last name and changing it to Alexander. We want you all to be able to have access to everything."

"All of this shit is crazy?" Gavin added.

"No. It's not. In the event we aren't available, we will need you all to handle shit," Prada spoke, staring dead at Gavin.

"We already handle shit for you all. I don't understand why we have to do this. I just signed papers with Fendi giving me access over everything.

"You all have to do it. No key players will fuck with you if you don't have that last name on paper," Ms. Gladys voiced as she flamed up a stanking ass black and mild.

"Should I be worried, Fendi?"

"Yeah, should I be worried, Givenchy? Lately, I've been feeling like something bad is going to happen. Is this why we have to do this?"

"I guess you not worried, huh Gavin?" Prada gritted at her.

He's a big mean ass nigga. I can't wait for her to fuck him up. He has been asking for it lately, around here acting like he's crazy. I told her she needs to bite a chunk out of his ass.

She needs to maul his ass like a Pitbull. Ever since I did that shit to Fendi, the nigga thinks twice. All it takes is one good time to fuck a nigga up to let him know not to play with you.

"I stay worried about your ass nigga. I'll gladly take your last name. Anything is better than being a Mills anyway." Gavin quickly signed the papers and pushed them away from her.

"When all of this is said and done. I better get the wedding of my fucking dreams. Do not play with me, Givenchy. Ms. Gladys, I'm holding you accountable for his actions. Since you're standing here vouching for this shit, you will get them to the altar." Miyani signed the papers and handed them to G.

That left me sitting there staring at Fendi's ass. He had this smug ass look on his face. The nigga just knew that I was going to sign the papers. Of course, I was going to sign the papers. Honestly, we were already looked at as being married to them. In the streets, we were addressed as Mrs. Alexander. I've watched these niggas beat niggas ass if they didn't refer to us as such, especially, Miyani. From the moment I met him, Givenchy has always referred to her as his wife. Prada and Fendi just started doing the shit. Sometimes I wonder if they really came from the same nut sack. They are all the same but extremely different if that makes any sense.

"Don't look at me like that, nigga! This signature is going to be your death sentence if you play with me. You already know I'm going ape shit behind my heart. Marriage or no marriage, you belong to me, nigga." I signed the papers and slid them across the table to his ass.

As if on cue, an uneasy feeling came over me that I couldn't explain. Just staring at Ms. Gladys, Givenchy, Prada, and Fendi, let me know some shit was about to kick off. I just hoped Miyani and Gavin were war ready. These motherfuckers are not just giving us their last name for nothing or moving us out to Atlanta, for that matter. It's a method behind all this fucking madness. I just prayed we all made it out of this shit on top.

A nigga felt fucked up sitting poolside with my son and daughter. Gavin hadn't come out to check on us or shit. This was the first weekend with my daughter spending the night under our roof. Gavin kept saying that she was cool and accepted it, but she sure had a funny way of showing it.

It's been proven that I knew nothing about having a

daughter, yet Gavin was acting as if I had cheated on her. I've apologized so many fucking times, but she is still giving me her ass to kiss. At this point, I don't know what to do.

On the bright side, she signed the paperwork to take my last name legally. After we solidify this deal in Panama, shit will go back to normal for the whole team. This shit needed to hurry up and get back right. The girls were starting to get anxious. Taking our last names and moving out to Atlanta was not sitting right with them. At the same time, my brothers and I hit the jackpot by making shit official with them.

As much as they hated what was going on, they were riding. That's why I needed my baby to forgive me. I can't focus on the street shit because shit ain't right at home. With everything going on, anything could happen. A nigga can't afford to get fucked up in these streets and be on bad terms with his lady. Right now, Gavin and I needed to be one band one sound around this motherfucker. All this silent treatment is starting to get on my last nerve. I'm not going to bed beefing with her ass another night. It's hard as hell for a nigga when she gets mad. Her ass be stingy with the pussy. She knows I'm nympho, and she uses that shit against me. That's how I know I love Gavin. Had she been any other bitch holding out on the pussy, I would have hopped in a couple of more pussies by now. Shit with her is different. Gavin makes me want to be different.

I've stopped popping pills and slowed up on my drinking. That shit was hurting her, so I changed. The least she could do is acknowledge the fact that a nigga did that. I'm not looking for brownie points because I did what a man is supposed to do. A man is supposed to change for the greater good of his family. Everything I'm doing right now is for Gavin and my kids. I can't afford for her to lose her faith in me. Even though I feel like I'm being punished at this point for nothing, I have to be the bigger person and fix this shit.

"ARE you going to hide up here in the room the whole time she's here?"

"I'm not hiding. I'm actually up here packing some things I'll need in Atlanta." Gavin was talking and walking in and out of our closet.

"Come here. Just have a seat for a minute so we can talk. We can't keep walking around here giving each other silent treatment. Aren't you tired of being mad at a nigga?" I pulled her into my embrace, and she was trying her best to get away from me.

"Come on now, Prada. You're going to make me forget something." Noticing that she was getting mad, I quickly let her go. Just that quick, I became frustrated as fuck with her.

"Fuck it! I give up." I threw my hands up in the air and walked out of the room. I quickly turned back around and went back inside. She jumped and hid something behind her back.

"What's that?" I asked, trying to see what she was hiding.

"It's nothing, Prada."

"A pregnancy test is a big ass something. What you pregnant? Let me find out you trying to kill my seed, Gavin. I swear I'm going to forget that I love your ass."

"Let my face go and calm down. As you can see, the test has never been opened. I was going to wait and take it. My period is a couple of days late, so it could be a false alarm. That's why I didn't tell you. It's just so much going on right now. I have so much going on right now, Prada." Gavin bussed out in tears, and that shit just made me grab her in my arms. I held her and let her get her cry out. Obviously, she had some shit on her heart.

"Shhhh! Stop crying. Tell your man what's wrong. I thought a baby was what we wanted. I know I fucked up not telling you about Tiyonni's existence. On some real shit, a nigga was scared to lose you. I can't change the fact that she's mine. If you're not ready, I won't bring her back here."

"No, Prada, your daughter has nothing to do with this. You have loved my son from the jump. How could I not accept your child? Come on now. You know me. Being a mom is my life."

"Then talk to me. We have to get down to the bottom of this shit. It doesn't matter if you're pregnant right now or not. I'm not going another day without getting back to the way we used to be. Just tell me what you need from me. How can I fix anything if you're not telling me what's wrong?"

"I need to know that I can trust you. You can't have me out here in these streets looking crazy. I've put my life and freedom on the line being with you. I don't need you shielding me from shit. Let me know what the fuck is going on so that I can make my own decisions. I'm not the same Gavin you met. The new me don't need to be rescued or babied. The shit I've been through has made me stronger than you think. I signed those papers because I love you. You have had the ability to lead me, so I have no problem with following you. Just lead me properly. For this to be successful, it requires a level of honesty and truthfulness. Yes, I know you like to shield me, but there is some shit I need to know about. There is no need to feel like you need to explain yourself. This is the last and final olive branch I'll extend before I just leave your ass. Don't tell me you're sorry, either. Just do better by me. Don't make me regret being with your ass okay, Prada. I'm tired of fighting. Let me take this pregnancy test, and we will go from there."

I attempted to respond, but she quickly held her hand up to stop me. All I could do was sit down and wait for her to come back out. Sometimes I wished Gavin were still my good girl. I managed to turn her into an angry black woman who is tired of my shit. Yeah, we needed to hurry up and make it back from Panama. It was time for me to really focus on what's important, and that's the family that I've created. After what seemed like forever, Gavin came out of the bathroom. She had on her poker face on, so I couldn't read her. Without hesitation, I stood to my feet, waiting for her to tell me the results.

"What does it say?"

"You want a boy or a girl." She handed me the pregnancy the test, and it read *positive* in the window.

"Man, it doesn't even matter. I just want it to be healthy. A nigga is just happy that we're finally pregnant. Let me get this shit handled in Panama. I swear when I get back, my focus is going to be on our family. I love you so much, Gavin."

"I love you too. Now stop worrying about us. You need to focus on helping G get Team Supreme back up and running. I'll be okay in Atlanta. Handle your shit, and don't disappoint me."

As Gavin grabbed my face and kissed me like I was going off to prison, it scared the fuck out of me for a minute. Things had shifted that fast. A nigga had no other choice but to handle this shit and get back home to my family.

FIFTEEN

MS. GLADYS

"What's good? Why you got us all over here? It ain't even Sunday?"

"I am not in the mood for your shit today, Fendi. Sit your ass down so we can discuss some shit. That goes for both of y'all as well."

I was so mad at my grandsons that I could kill them.

The shit I've just learned about what's going on has me livid. They've been moving on the chessboard without my fucking permission. That's that bullshit they know I do not fucking play about.

"Why all aggression?" Prada asked.

"That's what I'm trying to see? What's going on?" Looking at the smug ass look on Givenchy's face made me want to beat his ass. He's been doing that smart ass shit since he was a kid. I love, but I that he thinks he so goddamn smart.

"What's going on is the shit you all have been keeping from me? Why in the hell wasn't I informed about Nettie and Niara working with the government?"

"I'm going to kick Butta's ass! I should have known he was going to tell you."

"Shut the fuck up, Prada! Butta, ain't told me shit. Apparently, you niggas forgot that my name holds weight in this city. Before it was the Alexander Boys, it was Gladys Alexander. I ran the city by myself. Let's get some shit straight. I am the foundation of all things Supreme. There ain't shit that I should have to find out from the streets that compromise my fucking family. I'm lost as to why we're even having this conversation, especially since we decided that we would no longer keep each other out of the loop."

I grabbed my bottle of Jameson and sat down at the dining room table. These motherfuckers had my pressure through the roof. The only thing that would calm me down was a joint and me a shot.

"Yeah, we did agree to that. We all made an executive decision that it would be better if you didn't know, simply for the reason that you're bitching at us right now. You want to be on the battle lines with us, and that's not going to happen. Yes, without you, Team Supreme wouldn't be in existence. To be honest, if memory serves me right, you're retired. Do you remember you stepped down and gave me the key to the city?"

"Don't get cute with me, Givenchy. Yes, I'm retired, but I am still very much active. Don't let my retirement make you think I'm to be fucked with. That goes for all three of you. As the matriarch of this family, I deserve to know what the fuck is going on. Not only that, but I should know the moves that are about to be made.

I apologize if I make you feel like you can't handle it. Trust me. I would never have turned over the reins if you were incompetent. However, right now, I think you're making a big mistake by moving the family down to Atlanta. Team Supreme is Chicago. What the fuck is this family gone do down in the south? Yeah, we got nice ass business partnerships down there, but we can't go moving down there. We run this motherfucking city, and not even the government can change that!

"The move is not permanent granny. It's just until we can get this shit taking care of." Fendi argued.

"I understand all that, but since when y'all start operating with fear! You niggas have fallen in love and forgot about who runs this motherfucker. Now let me school y'all on some shit. Miyani, Gavin, and Dream do not want to go to no fucking Atlanta. The only reason they're even agreeing to go is to please you all.

"You make it sound like that's a bad thing," Prada said as he poured himself a shot of D'ussé.

"It will become a bad thing. You don't always want your women to agree with shit to make you happy. In the end, she will grow old, bitter, and resentful. Now I don't know if y'all paying attention, but them three are not innocent these days. They also aren't fools. Miyani just proved to us that she could hold her own. I've seen Gavin and Dream in action too. Trust me. They can handle themselves just fine here in the Chi. They take being a part of Team Supreme very seriously, so you guys leaving them out of the loop will have them taking matters into their own hands. I mean, after all, they've been groomed in the *Art of War* courtesy of Team Supreme.

Have I ever steered you boys in the wrong direction when it comes down to business? Don't send them girls down to know damn Atlanta. Also, you need to open Team Supremes' operations back up. We've lost damn near five million in one week. That's way too much."

"I was cool with not sending them to the A, but resuming operations is risky," Givenchy spoke.

"I agree with G. Let's cancel the moving plans, but the shutdown should stay that way. At least until we handle Nettie and Niara. Now Team Supreme has two major business ventures coming up. We can't afford to not be focused. This Bosses Roundtable and Panama connection are big for the family. Not many people are getting accepted into these types of factions. Just being considered is big. Trust me. Thug Inc. is watching your every move. General Idris is watching your every move. Team Supreme needs to resume operations today and not a minute after."

"What happens when we open up and the FEDS finally make their move?" Fendi asked.

"If they were going to move in, they would have been moved in. Let's tie up these loose ends and recoup the money we lost. Get our people back on the street ASAP! I know this situation with Nettie is touchy for you, Givenchy, so let me handle her and Niara. I need my boys out here taking Team Supreme to a new level. Make sure this is the last time you leave me out of the loop. Save yourself the grief of hearing my fucking mouth. I know everything, even when you think I don't know shit. Remember united we stand and divided we fall. Let's all work together instead of around each other. Now that that's out of the way... congratulations! I'm so happy for you guys!"

I rushed over and wrapped my arms around Prada. It warmed my heart to know that Gavin was finally pregnant.

"Thanks, granny."

"Congratulations, bro!" Both Fendi and Givenchy said in unison while exchanging a warm hug with him.

Moments like this make me feel like Chanel should be here. No matter what these are still the children she birthed. After the shit that nigga Joffery pulled, I've washed my hands with Chanel. I don't care what she says. That man is not lying on her. The fact that she is still dodging me lets me know she did offer up her own grandchild. Any time she can't face me, her ass is guilty.

This whole set up with Chanel is still something I don't understand. So, many years I wished that my daughter were alive. When I found out that she was alive, I praised God. However, the way she be moving makes me wish her ass had never come back. These boys have worked hard to become the men that they are. I watched them hurt for years after her death. She came here and got their hopes up of having their momma back only for the selfish ass bitch to leave them again. Daughter or no daughter, she can stay the fuck away from me. She can stay her ass in Haiti with all that sneaky shit. I'm just glad Versace and that baby is here with us. If she wants to be the damn Queen of Coke, she can go right ahead. Her thirst for power will not interfere with what the fuck we got going on here. It's Team Supreme, and it ain't no in-between.

"WHAT'S GOOD, Ms. Gladys? Long time no see," Nettie stumbled over her words as she spoke. It was obvious my presence had her shook. Honestly, the bitch should be. She snaked her neck around to see if anyone was with me.

"Don't worry. I came alone. Can I come in, or do I have to stand out here in the cold?" She was blocking me from walking straight in her shit. However, she knows she had no choice but to let me inside.

"What brings you here?" she quizzed.

I became disgusted observing her. The bitch looked like life hadn't treated her fairly. Gone was the flashy ass Nettie Boo I looked at like one of my own. Although I was there to kill her, it still hurt my heart. We took her in and groomed her. The snake shit she did to us hurt. The thing that has me the most upset is how she moved with Givenchy. She did it without a care that he would find out. That's because she knew he wouldn't murk her behind no pussy at that time. He's a real ass nigga, and his grandma taught him well. At the same time, I take it personally when someone hurts him the way she did. Givenchy spared her life, and Ms. Gladys is going to snatch it the fuck away.

"Before I tell you why I'm here. Where is Niara? She needs to be present for this." I sat down on the loveseat across from Nettie. She was sitting on the couch, all slouched over and looking pitiful as fuck.

"Niara ain't here, and I don't know where the bitch at!"

"She left your ass, huh?" I couldn't do shit but laugh. Nettie was sick as hell about it. The forty ounces of beer she was chugging showed it. Anybody chugging a beer the way she is, definitely got some shit going on with them.

"If you came here to throw up in my face, you can

leave!" Before that bitch ever knew what happened, I had jumped up and sliced her ass across the face with my blade.

"Ahhhhhhhhh!" She had fallen over on the couch and then onto the floor. The blood was practically shooting out the side of her face.

"You forgot who the fuck you talking to! Bitch, you think you gone tell me how to behave in your shit after you betrayed my family. All of this over some part-time dyke that couldn't keep a dick out of her mouth to save her life. You betrayed my grandson behind a bitch he didn't give not one fuck about. Did you think we wouldn't find out it was you and that bitch snitching? Not only are you disloyal, but your ass is a rat. You and I both know how Team Supreme feels about rats. Give me one motherfucking reason why I shouldn't slice your fucking throat."

"Pleaseeee, Ms. Gladys! I'm so sorry. I didn't know that bitch was snitching. She used me to get back at Givenchy. You've got to believe me. I've never been a rat. I swear to God. Just let me get to the hospital. If you give me a chance, I swear I'll leave town and never come back. Please, Ms. Gladys!" The bitch was struggling, but little did she know the shit was all in vain.

"The thing about second chances is you don't get one. Team Supreme requires you to act accordingly the first time around. See you in hell, rat!"

I roughly grabbed her by the head and yanked her head back. Without hesitation, I sliced her ass from ear-to-ear, making sure to cut the carotid artery. Usually, I don't stick around and wait to see people take their last breath, but this was different, though. I needed to make sure that the bitch was dead, that, and the satisfaction of seeing how nice I still was with that blade.

VERSACE

Exhausted wasn't the word for the way I was feeling. I had thrown two parties in one day, and all I wanted to do was get home and lay it down. Being an event planner is all fun and games until your ass is double booked and worn the fuck out. The money is everything because I only deal with upscale clients. Today showed me that I indeed needed to hire assistants to work for me. I'm a perfectionist, so I like to do everything myself. I'm going to have to put some faith in someone else for the help I needed. I've been so exhausted that I haven't had a lot of time with my son. I didn't take on any events for this upcoming week. Since everybody is now staying in Chicago, I plan on catching up with them.

My brothers have been knee-deep in trying to keep the team out of jail. A couple of times, when Fendi came over to the house, I overheard him and Dex talking. Things were far deeper than they had been letting on. A part of me was worried that they might be headed to prison. The other part knew that they would beat the fucking pigs trying to take them down. In the short time that I have gotten to know my brothers. I've come to the realization that they are beasts at what they do in these streets. If it's anyone in this world that can beat the system, Team Supreme definitely can.

I'll just be glad when all this shit is over. My sisters-in-law are no fun when they are trying to hold my brothers down. They be on straight business when it comes down to Alexander Enterprises. I watched Prada act a damn fool with Gavin, but not once did she lack in her duties with the family business. The same goes for Miyani and Dream. They love my brothers. They had better marry them girls after all this shit is over. Fuck rocking their last names. Put that shit on paper, nigga. Without a doubt, I know that they will marry them. My brothers are a unique type of breed. Niggas not out here turning all their assets over to females the way they are. You got to be a powerful bitch to get a man do what they're doing.

Hell, they'll probably go down as the first hood niggas in history to give females their last name without walking down a damn aisle. Team Supreme is on another level. I bet money it's not another group of niggas out here that can fuck with my brothers.

I pray all their troubles will be over soon. From the moment I've met them, it's always been them against the world. They're good-hearted men with some good-hearted women who love them. They really do deserve a break to just live and enjoy the fruits of the labor.

"It looks like life here in Chicago is treating you well," the sound of Joffery's voice made me quickly turn around and lock eyes with him. Immediately, I started panicking, looking at him holding a gun down to his side.

"What the fuck do you want from me?" I was looking around for Dexter but remembered he was outside waiting for me to come out.

"I want my son. You can stop looking for your little friend. He's out front struggling to breathe from the bullet I put in his chest. Now take me to get my fucking son!" Joffery yelled while aiming his gun at me.

"You might as well kill me right now! For the sake and safety of my son, I'll never subject him to being with you or your fucked-up family!"

"Why the fuck you want to make this shit so difficult? You bring your ass out here to this ghetto ass city and change on me. What happened to you?"

"What happened to me is that I found my voice. Back in Haiti, I had my father and my mother making lifelong decisions for me. I admit, at one time, I loved you more than anything."

I stopped talking when he swiftly moved toward me. Joffery's big, tall frame damn near swallowed me whole. Although he had never been violent with me, I've watched him be violent with others. I hated to admit, but he had my ass a little shook. At the same time, I wasn't backing down from his ass. He's going to have to kill me. I'll never willingly hand over my son to his ass.

"So, what are you saying? You don't love your husband."

"My husband was married to another woman last time I checked. No! I do not love you. If memory serves me right, you chose Haiti over your son. You showed up eight months later trying to take him. Nigga, is you retarded? Do you actually think that I would be with a person who moves like that? Why are you here, Joffery?"

"That nigga got you feeling herself, huh? You think I don't know you fucking that bitch ass nigga. That's why I killed his ass. Since I can't have my son, I might as well kill your bitch ass too."

Before I could respond, Joffery wrapped his hands around my neck and tried to choke the life out of me. I was starting to see spots as he squeezed harder and harder. I heard a gunshot go off right before everything went black.

I QUICKLY SAT up in bed and tried to focus. The dream I just had seemed so damn real. Looking around my bedroom, I realized I didn't remember falling to sleep. The pain I felt in my neck made me shoot up out of bed. Panic sat in as I rushed out of the room and into my son's room. I breathed a sigh of relief, seeing him asleep in his bed. I placed a kiss on his forehead and stared at him while I caught my breath.

"Ahhhhhhhh!" Hearing a male's voice screaming made me rush out the room. My mind immediately went to Dexter.

That's when the dream started replaying vividly in my head. The shit wasn't a dream. It had actually happened. As I rushed passed the living room, I stopped in my tracks. I couldn't help but lose all my stomach contents at the sight of all the blood. Dexter was laid out on top of my living room table, bloody as hell. Givenchy, Prada, and Fendi were standing over him dressed like surgeons. I couldn't believe my eyes. My brothers were removing bullets out of him.

"Go back upstairs now!" Givenchy yelled.

"Nooo! Take him to the hospital!"

"We can't take him to the hospital. He's gone be straight! Go back upstairs right now!" Prada gritted.

"This is all my fault. I should have just gone back to Haiti."

"This shit ain't your fault. Go back upstairs. We stitching him up now. Dex gone be good," Fendi's voice calmed me, and I slowly walked back up the stairs.

Before going back into my room, I grabbed my son. I was scared to death. Dex looked like he had passed out or checked out. I'll never forgive myself if he dies. Why in the hell didn't I just go back to Haiti? It's my fault why Joffery came here in the first place. This shit was not a good feeling. The scene back at the club vividly played in my mind. The last thing I remember was hearing a gunshot and looking into Joffery's dark black eyes.

"You good, sis?" Givenchy asked as he walked into my room.

"Not really. The last thing I remember is hearing a gunshot before I passed out. Joffery was trying to kill me.

"Well, you ain't got to worry about that motherfucker no more! I put a bullet in the back of his head when I walked in on him choking you. All night I had been having an uneasy feeling, so I got out of bed to come check shit out. Thank God I came. If I hadn't, you and Dex would be dead. We got the bullet out of his chest, and he's going to have to stay here until he heals. We can't move him right now. Do you think you can look out for him? We got some shit that must get handled, and we can't sit over here with him. A nurse will also move in to do the hard parts. Dream just made it. She's going to stay with you too. Stop tripping and blaming yourself. Think about it like this. You don't have to worry about that motherfucker anymore. Can you look after Dex while we're gone?

"Yeah, I can. Thank you so much. I owe you my life."

"Oh! Stop it! I did what big brothers are supposed to do. When we get back from this business trip, you need to go to the gun range. G reached over and hugged me before leaving the room.

Although it made me feel good to know that Dexter was going to be okay, I still felt terrible. I'm just glad Joffery is gone. It killed me knowing that my son would never have his father. Having said that, he'll never miss someone he never knew anyway.

IT HAD BEEN a week since the shooting, and Dex was getter better. Getting better meant that he was being a pain in my ass. For the last week, I've been waiting on him hand and foot. I felt bad about him getting shot on the account of me. However, it's check-out time. If he stays in this house with me one more second, I'm going to shoot and kill his ass myself. Dream needs to come and get her fucking brother.

"What the hell took you so long? You didn't hear my bell?"

"If you ring that motherfucker again, I'm going to smash it with a hammer. What the hell do you want, Dex?"

"I wanted you to hand me that remote."

"Are you serious right now?" This nigga had lost his damn mind. The remote was sitting inches away from him in the bed. All his black ass had to do was reach up and grab it.

"You gone hand the remote to me or not?"

"I'm not handing you shit. Get your ass up and get it your damn self. Your ass is up and getting around one hundred percent compared to last week this time. It's time for you to take your ass home and take that damn nurse with you!"

I walked out of the guest bedroom and slammed the door hard as hell. Givenchy was going to have to be mad at me because I was done.

Dex had been a pain in my ass with all the damn demands he had. One wouldn't think how he damn near death a week ago. I don't know what my brothers did, but they stitched his ass up good as hell. Now that he's recovered, there is no need for him to be here.

"Why you treating a nigga like that? I take a bullet for you, and that's how you do me." Dex said as he walked inside the kitchen.

I couldn't respond because my words had got caught up in my throat. He was shirtless and only rocking a pair of Versace underwear. The sight of the bandages on his chest didn't take away from his physique. Of course, he had dropped some pounds from being shot, but it didn't take shit away from the beautiful sight before me.

"I'm tired of your ass. Nigga, I am not your maid. I've been waiting on your ass hand and foot cause I feel responsible, but nigga, I'm not the damn help. You better play that shit with your nurse. I am not the one, Dexter!"

"Damn, say my name like that again."

"Boy, if you don't get the fuck outta my face."

He was now all up in my personal space. I was gently pushing him back, trying not to hurt his wounds. Lowkey I wanted him to stay right up on me. The nigga's dick was poking me on my leg a little. For the first time, I felt attracted to him.

"Your body is telling me something different. Touch him. He doesn't bite unless you want him to."

"Nah! I don't want him to. Put that thing away before my brothers kill your ass."

"Girl, you know you want all this sexy chocolate. As far as your brothers go, they know how I feel. Now come change my bandages. Your hands soft ass fuck." Dex licked his lips and waited for me to follow him.

"If I didn't know any better, I would say you just mind fucked me."

"I jack my dick every night at the very thought of you!"

I couldn't hold my composure. Listening to Dexter say that with a straight face had me dying laughing. Had he been any other nigga, I would have gone the fuck off, but this shit was hilarious.

"Nigga, your ass is nasty."

"Hell yeah! I'm a nasty ass nigga. The ladies call me Nasty Dex with the Best Sex. You'll find out about me, though. That's another hood love story for another book," he stated matter-of-factly.

"Nigga, please! Come on so I can change your bandages."

Dex had lost his damn mind talking that slick shit. These Chicago niggas swear they got all the game in the world. Dex really has to get out of my house now. I got a feeling he will talk me right up out of my damn panties. That's the last thing I needed was to take things to another level with him. That nigga's crazy and fine as hell, but he gives me toxic ass nigga vibes. After what the fuck I've been through, the last thing I need is another toxic nigga in my damn life.

SEVENTEEN
MIYANI

Givenchy would go ballistic when he finds out what I've been up to. I felt bad at first, but knowing what I know now, I have no regrets. From the moment I stepped out of jail, my man has been different. I'm used to him being my strong one, so it's hard for me to see him like this. These people got my man out here doubting who the fuck he is. He puts on a good façade, but that shit doesn't work with me. I've watched him toss and turn every night behind this shit. Givenchy is the rock of this family, and everything rests on his shoulders. Seeing him so overwhelmed made me spring into action.

My baby never asks for much. All he wants is for Team Supreme to be successful as fuck, which it is. At the same time, there are government officials who feel different — just thinking about how this shit has played out fucks with me.

Givenchy gives to so many charities across this city. He has built a shelter for the homeless and given them jobs so they can get on their feet. These motherfuckers need to stop playing with my baby and make him mayor.

"I'm sorry, ma'am. You can't go in there. A meeting is in session."

"I know. I'm supposed to be at this meeting. I'm just running late." I quickly rushed past the pencil-thin elderly woman as she rushed behind me. My ass just breached all the damn security checkpoints at the State building to get to Governor Braggs' office.

It was quite easy, especially since Malcolm had left me his security clearance badge. I just knew the damn thing would not work with him being dead and all. To my surprise, it worked at every entry. I just needed to get into this fucking meeting and get the hell out of dodge.

"I'm so sorry, Governor. She rushed past me."

His body tensed up as he saw me enter the room. I walked right in front of him and held my phone up to his face. He fell in line just like I knew he would. Watching himself tied up in all black leather with a dildo up his ass shut him up quick. It was game the fuck on, and I would be the only one walking out a winner.

"It's fine, Clarissa."

"What is the meaning of this? Who is this woman? She is not a government official and should not be in here during this time."

As she talked that cash money shit, I went in search of the picture I needed to show her. This one was especially humiliating.

"I'm Malcolm Mills' daughter. Does your husband know you used to meet with my dad to give him rim jobs? Sit your ass down and shut the fuck up." I shoved the phone in her face, and she quickly stood down. All that rah-rah shit she was just on had disappeared. She was unraveling right before me. I had shown her a video of her eating my father's ass. The shit was sick as fuck. Who knew he was into that nasty shit? Looking at the tape, she thoroughly enjoyed doing the shit.

"What is the meaning of all this? I came here for the quarterly report. Not for some gangster's wife to walking around like she owns this place."

"I'm flattered you know who I am. That gangster you speak of will murder you and your entire family. I advise your cracker ass to talk to my nice, especially, since you're the one who placed those bricks of coke in my trunk."

Mike Monroe had played a major role in my arrest, along with Governor Bragg and the State's Attorney, Andrea Myers. That's why I'm here now. It's time for these motherfuckers to pay the piper.

"I don't have to listen to this craziness. I will not be bribed by the likes of you."

"You're going to do whatever the fuck I want you to do. Now what I should be doing is killing you motherfuckers for playing with my life and freedom. I'm not going to do that, though. I come bearing gifts. Reaching inside of my purse, I pulled out three envelopes and handed one to each of them.

"Why do we have bank papers?" the states' attorney asked.

"Each of those accounts has two million in it and is in your names."

"Wait a minute. Why are you giving us two million dollars?" Governor Bragg asked.

"Not too long ago, Givenchy came and had a sit-down with you. I know you all remember the conversation that day he came in here and asked for your endorsement for mayor. Of course, that's when the brilliant plan came up for you motherfuckers to teach him a lesson. That lesson was planting bricks in my car so that I could be arrested. I'm sure you know that I was assaulted and slashed in the face, not to mention I lost a baby I didn't even know I was carrying. Had I not been in jail, those things never would have happened."

"Givenchy left us no choice. He came in here making demands."

"Didn't I tell you to shut the fuck up? Now listen to me and pay close attention. I'm giving you each two million dollars now for Givenchy's endorsement for mayor. Once he is elected, I will place two million more in each of your accounts.

"What if we don't want to agree to this?"

"Don't agree and find out. Agree and try to cross me, your children will find out. I don't give a fuck about you or your family. Obviously, you don't give a fuck about mine. I'm not here to threaten you. I will follow through with everything I've said today. I'm simply here to make sure my man becomes mayor. The money becomes available the moment you agree. The bloodshed begins the moment you disagree. The ball is in your court."

"We will agree, but you have to get rid of the shit you have against us!" Governor Bragg stated.

"I'll destroy it when my husband is the Mayor of Chicago. Now make me proud. Our first campaign meeting is the first of next month. Nice doing business with you all."

I walked out with my head so far up in the air. I knew G was going to be mayor when the next election took place. Coming here was a risk, but it was one that I'm willing to take. For Givenchy, I'll lay my life on the line. He's given me the world, so it's only right I work to create the world he desires. Givenchy Alexander doesn't have shit to worry about as long as he got me.

"OHHHHHH, yesssss! Just like that! I'm about to cum all over that big ass dick!" I moaned as I rocked back and forth on his dick. We had been fucking all night, and Givenchy would be getting ready to head to Panama soon. He hadn't even left yet, and I was missing him.

"That's right cum all over this dick!" Givenchy roughly grabbed me by the waist and slammed me up and down roughly.

With each thrust, it felt like he was touching my soul and taking a little of me with him. My baby was fucking me like he had a point to prove. Little did he know he had proven his point five nuts ago. Usually, he would pull out, but I didn't want him to. I allowed him to let off in the pussy. The shit was feeling too good for me not to. We had been being extremely cautious because I wasn't on birth control.

That shit had started me to gain weight. There was no way I was about to be walking around big as hell. I'm a fanatic about my weight, so it's a must I keep it under control.

After coming, we fucked a couple more times until it was time for him to get dressed for his flight.

I laid across the bed, watching him prepare to head to the airstrip. For the first time in a long time, he was happier. No longer did his face bear a look of worry. He seemed to be more so content and happy. Team Supreme had been back up and running with no issues. Getting to the club in time to save Versace and Dex was another reason he was in such a better mood. This business trip to Panama is supposed to solidify a better drug transportation system between countries. Once he handles the situation out there, he can get prepared for the Bosses Roundtable event. I think I'm more excited to attend then he is.

"How long will you be out in Panama?"

"Hopefully, this shit only takes a day or two. Gianna is going to kill me if I miss her recital. In the event that I don't be back in time, make sure you record."

"I will, baby. Man, I hope you can make it back in time. She's going to be so disappointed if you can't make it."

"What about you? Will you be disappointed if I don't make it back?"

"You haven't even left, and I'm in my feelings. Just promise me that you're going to be safe and make it back home to us."

"I promise, beautiful. My car is outside. I'll call you when we land in a couple of hours. You girls be good while we're gone."

"I'm always good." I laughed slyly.

"Yeah, aight. I love you, Miyani Alexander."

"I love you too, Givenchy Alexander."

He leaned over the bed, and we engaged in a passionate kiss. I don't know what came over me, but I wrapped my arms around him tight. For some reason, I didn't want him to go, but I knew he had to. It took everything in me not to tell him to stay. His brothers could solidify the deal. Then again, they would probably end up in a shootout. It was best he handled that shit and came on back home. That's when I'm going to come clean about my meeting. All that fucking we did had a bitch exhausted.

Not long after Givenchy left, I finally dozed off, only to be awakened by someone banging on my front door. Half asleep, I sat up and tried to focus. I wasn't sure what the fuck was going on, so I quickly cut on the security screen. The sight of two police officers made me throw on my robe. I damn near fell trying to get down the stairs. Both Gianna and G-Baby were right behind me as I raced to the door.

"Yes!" I answered the door, out of breath.

"Are you Miyani Alexander?"

"Yes, I am. Is there something wrong, officer?"

"I'm sorry to inform you, but your husband's plane crashed about ten minutes after takeoff earlier this morning. Everyone aboard the aircraft is believed to have perished."

"Nooooo! Maybe you made a mistake. Nothing is wrong with my husband. He's gone on a business trip. He'll be back in a couple of days. You see, our daughter has a very important recital, and he has to attend it. If he doesn't, she will be so disappointed. So, you see, he can't be dead." Tears started to pour out of my eyes because this man was lying to me.

"I'm sorry for your loss, Mrs. Alexander." The officer tipped his hat and walked away.

I collapsed right there in the foyer of my house. I let out

a blood-curdling scream that scared the fuck out of my kids. They ran to my side and hugged me.

"You lied to me! You promised me you were coming back home! How could you do this to me? Oh, God! Please help me!"

"Come on, Miyani!" Looking up at Butta and Gunna crying like babies let me know this wasn't a dream. Givenchy, Prada, and Fendi were dead!

COMING SOON!!!

Hood Supreme 5

* 9 7 9 8 6 6 7 9 7 1 9 2 4 *